T0362789

THEA WELSH

THE STORY OF THE YEAR OF 1912
IN THE VILLAGE OF ELZA DARZINS

*un*tapped

ABOUT *UNTAPPED*

Most Australian books ever written have fallen out of print and become unavailable for purchase or loan from libraries. This includes important local and national histories, biographies and memoirs, beloved children's titles, and even winners of glittering literary prizes such as the Miles Franklin Literary Award.

Supported by funding from state and territory libraries, philanthropists and the Australian Research Council, *Untapped* is identifying Australia's culturally important lost books, digitising them, and promoting them to new generations of readers. As well as providing access to lost books and a new source of revenue for their writers, the *Untapped* collaboration is supporting new research into the economic value of authors' reversion rights and book promotion by libraries, and the relationship between library lending and digital book sales. The results will feed into public policy discussions about how we can better support Australian authors, readers and culture.

See untapped.org.au for more information, including a full list of project partners and rediscovered books.

Readers are reminded that these books are products of their time. Some may contain language or reflect views that might now be found offensive or inappropriate.

AUTHOR'S NOTE

The Sydney Film Festival is held in June every year, the Cannes Film Festival in May. Erika Cavanagh's story spans a period of eighteen months: it begins on a hot summer day in Sydney in January, proceeds to the time of the Sydney Film Festival and ends the following May, in Cannes.

This is the *only* factual basis for Erika's story. Everything else is pure fiction. As they say in other books, all the characters are entirely fictitious and there is no reference to any living person.

The only other items which are not fictitious in this book are the excerpts from letters which appear at the beginning of each of the novel's three parts. These excerpts are reproduced here courtesy of the *Sydney Morning Herald*. I am also indebted to the authors of the letters for their kind permission.

I also wish to thank Rose Creswell and Philippe Tanguy and to gratefully acknowledge the assistance of the Literature Board of the Australia Council.

This book is dedicated to Tim, Adrienne, Colin and Richard.

Thea Welsh
Sydney
1990

CONTENTS

PART ONE
COLD WAR BABY

KINGS AND QUEENS

SIR: How long are the 'women's libbers' going to put up with Kings beating Queens as they do at all card games, from poker to bridge?

J Baird

(from the correspondence columns of the
Sydney Morning Herald)

CHAPTER 1

When Balodis died I was in London. I heard the news—a couple of brief sentences—on the radio in my hotel room. The next morning I went down to the street where I bought a copy of every newspaper on the stand. I stayed in the wind reading them. The items were usually headed: 'Soviet Film Director Dies.'

All the reports were based on the same news release datelined 8 May 1987. Soon I was sifting through each slight change of phrasing and discarding each small addition and reading the same announcement, again and again.

> *The Soviet film director, Peteris Balodis, died in Moscow yesterday following heart surgery. He was forty-six. Born in Latvia, Balodis became famous for three films he made about peasant life in Latvia before the Russian Revolution. His best-known film,* The Story of the Year of 1912 in the Village of Elza Darzins, *has won a number of international awards. Prior to his death, Balodis was directing a film which was set in the Ukraine.*

In the following months, articles about Balodis began to appear in the film press. These outlined the little that was known of his early career and gave lengthy descriptions of his works and the critical acclaim that they had received. But the accounts of his final days were as scanty as those of his early years. No-one seemed to know much about the film that he was making when he died, although it was commonly said to be about the life of a peasant soldier. There were rumours that he had made another film which had never been released. One report stated that after making *Elza's Story* (as everyone now calls *The Story of the Year of 1912 in the Village of Elza Darzins*) he'd started two other films—subjects unknown—which had both been abandoned and that he had intended his latest film to be the beginning of a trilogy about the life of Lenin. I thought this was unlikely, but I was intrigued by the idea. Balodis was always fond of trilogies.

His last years seemed to be all rumours and speculation. I heard more of these than anyone because people would always apply to me for information. I'd point out to them that I had spent most of my life on the other side of the world and implied that therefore I knew little about Balodis and even less about his producer, Leblenis. But still they kept coming. After all, my name was closely linked to his greatest film. Some of them were so persistent that I wondered if they had heard something— perhaps nothing precise that would enable them to ask a direct question—but enough to make them feel there was a lot more I could tell them.

At the time though I had made a resolution that the film came first and that I would never do anything to cause specu- lation or controversy about it. I had told myself, there are dan- gers in starting to tell a story. I might begin with Balodis's, but wouldn't I end up telling my own?

Then history caught up with me. A distant little country that had been forty years in obscurity was suddenly in the news. There were headlines about Latvia demanding its freedom. The reforms started in Moscow and then a few years later, the Union of Soviet Socialist Republics—the great power that so dominates this story—was gone. Its subject states, including the three Baltic countries Latvia, Lithuania and Estonia, were independent nations. In the years afterwards, when so many more dangerous secrets were being revealed, there seemed no reason why I should not recount my own.

Yet those dramatic changes which happened so quickly made the past seem unreal so that now when I go back to the beginning and I'm sitting in Louise's apartment reading the paper, with my back resolutely to the blue and brilliant harbour, I feel as though I'm composing the scene, looking around for the convincing detail, rather than reporting what actually happened in Sydney one hot summer.

But perhaps I would have felt this way in any case. Because I've always made up stories.

I was reading the paper that morning, looking for work, although I'd recently been offered a teaching position by the New South Wales Department of Education.

'Where?' asked Louise when I announced this news.

'The country,' I said.

Louise, with her gold hair and her red lips and purple fingernails, was so urban a figure it seemed pointless to get specific about the vast stretches of the continent.

'Didn't they tell you where in the country?'

'Gulargambone.'

She was putting in her earrings.

'Where's that?'

'In the north-west.'

'Have you been there?'

'I've been through it.'

'What's it like?'

'Its name is the best thing about it.'

My parents, however, thought I was very fortunate.

'There are not so many jobs,' my mother wrote, her large, round, unaccustomed hand grinding into the paper. 'You are being very lucky. You will be a good teacher. You have been having all the education yourself. This is a good town your father says. It is hot in summer and cold in winter. You will be buying a good coat. It will be thick.'

She had learnt English on her arrival in Australia and she spoke it well, but until I left home the only experience she'd

ever had of writing it had been to record her recipes. Her letters were couched in the same style: 'You will be having the two
eggs. You will be having the butter and the sugar. They will be
mixed. You will be adding the two eggs. They will be beaten.'

My mother was right about the job market. At the time, em-
ployers used to write to unsuccessful job seekers: 'All applicants
were of a high calibre.' This reassured us and also gently reminded us that we were far too numerous. We were glutting the
market with our high calibre.

If I'd been realistic that morning I would have admitted to
myself that only a local catastrophe was going to keep me out
of Gulargambone. But I'm not realistic. And what I was doing
was reading the positions vacant for shipping clerks and ticket
writers.

During months of scanning the employment pages I'd actually become attached to the notices of vacancies for shipping
clerks and ticket writers. The jobs themselves sounded like
definite and substantial pastimes. The advertisements never
called for displays of special qualities. They never required
leadership, initiative or drive. It was sufficient to have been,
once before, a shipping clerk or a ticket writer ... and to wish
to be one again. As I read the vacancies I used to imagine quiet
amiable people who were shipping clerks and ticket writers
leading quiet satisfied lives and changing jobs every few years
so as to keep a steady turnover in the papers.

I was finding it hard, though, to keep these shipping clerks
and ticket writers' lives static and contented. I was watching
a lot of daytime television serials at the time, and drama kept
creeping in.

'Having any luck?'

Louise was finally out of bed. It was nearly midday. As
I turned to say hello, she was opening the doors onto the

balcony and drawing the curtains. Immediately the room was very bright; and in that brilliant light Louise, with her messy gold hair and her orange kimono, should have looked garish. Instead, as usual, she looked as if the spectacular backdrop of blue sky and harbour had been designed for her. Hunched over the newspapers in my faded shirt and cotton skirt, I felt outscaled and smaller than life.

But I was used to having that reaction to Louise. I'd first met her when a mutual friend had arranged for me to move into her apartment and I was very conscious of the differences between us. She was a glamorous actress of thirty-three who had become famous at the age of seventeen as the star of a popular revue. I was twenty-three, I was an aspiring writer who had never written a word—except in my diary—and now I was to be employed as a teacher in Gulargambone. Normally I was so eager not to impose that I moved about the apartment like somebody keeping out of the sightlines of the windows. I discreetly tidied up the messes that Louise was constantly creating. And above all I fended off, as best I could, her occasional periods of intense interest in me.

This was the most unexpected—and unnerving—aspect of sharing an apartment with Louise. I had been prepared for everything else: the constant socialising, the many admirers, even the chocolates. Louise loved chocolates and was always being bought them as gifts. Sometimes she had so many admirers that the apartment seemed equally full of chocolates and men. But her interest in me was astonishing.

It was sincere. I used to think that she regarded me as a singularly deserving case; looking back, I realise I was wrong. Louise and I simply operated socially from different premises. *I* made friends slowly, working through all stages beginning with slight acquaintance and advancing gradually to intimacy and trust. But Louise, if *she* liked someone, treated them immediately with almost as much affection and concern as if she'd grown up with them. She soon saw that I needed 'encouragement', and so she proceeded to give it.

This was in spite of the fact that Louise, herself, while leading a glamorous life, was not much more successful in her career. Like most actors she was chronically 'between jobs'. In the past fortnight she had auditioned for more roles than I'd attended interviews all summer. Nonetheless, she was always confident.

'There doesn't seem to be much,' I said, casting a last glance at the shipping clerks and ticket writers' columns and then folding the newspaper.

As soon as I'd spoken I knew I'd made a mistake. This was precisely the sort of negative statement that Louise most disapproved of.

She said, thoughtfully: 'I think it might be a good idea, Erika, if *I* were to read the employment section. I think it depresses you and that affects your confidence.'

It's one thing to know you're having difficulty finding a job, but it's another altogether to be told that you are incapable of even looking for one in the newspaper.

My cheeks began to warm, but Louise had already picked up the paper and started reading.

'How come you missed this one?' she asked.

I looked at where her finger was pointing. It was one of those advertisements in a box by itself with a black line around it. It said:

'State Film Board of New South Wales.'

I should have known Louise's eyes would home in on anything to do with films. The New South Wales State Film Board, the advertisement stated, wanted a translator. Fluent in English and Latvian.

'You could do that!' Louise exclaimed.

'They wouldn't take me. I've had no professional experience,' I began, with the full knowledge that Louise was already drawing herself up for battle. So I went on: 'There are plenty of professional Latvian interpreters around. I think they even have a bureau.'

'Why are they advertising the job then? Why don't they apply straight to the bureau for a Latvian?'

I shrugged. 'Statutory requirements, perhaps? Like advertising Government tenders.'

This was improvised, but sounded feasible. Feeling victorious, I went into the kitchen to make some coffee.

When I returned Louise had prepared her arguments. She'd accepted unquestioningly all the information I'd supplied, but none of this interfered with her assessment of the situation. The job was ideal for me. Not only had it turned up in the nick of time, but it was exactly what I needed. It would provide me with opportunities, an *entrée* into the world of film, contacts, ideas for future advancement. Louise's knowledge of the State Film Board was sketchy, but she knew people who worked there and she assured me that once I was inside the doors of such an organisation my future was as good as made. 'The hardest part in film and theatre is always getting the first job. But once you've got that ...'

She never enquired if I was actually *interested* in working in films. She would probably have thought the question redundant. In Sydney at that time, everyone seemed to be dreaming of getting into the film industry. Every literate person was planning to write scripts. Every waiter in town was taking acting classes. Every taxi driver was a technician moonlighting between shoots. Ten years before, the Australian film industry had scarcely existed—but now it seemed as if all the city was one vast set for a musical in which the whole population leapt to their feet and jumped from out behind their office desks, workbenches and shop counters and declared that they wanted to be! That they were getting ready to be! That they were going to be ... in the movies!

This general aspiration didn't exercise any influence upon me that morning. Louise still needed to convince me. I tried to explain to her why I wouldn't be an adequate translator.

'My idiom would be out of date. I learnt the language from

my mother alone, and she left Latvia years ago.'

Louise dealt with *this* objection most efficiently.

'They can't be wanting you to translate *into* Latvian, otherwise someone in Latvia would be doing it. This must be *from* Latvian into English—and you've got a good English degree. In any case you must be able to express yourself adequately in Latvian or you wouldn't use it in your diary.'

I had forgotten that Louise knew about my diary. As long as my mother never saw it, my entries written in Latvian were as secret and secure as if they'd been written in a war-time code.

'But there are cultural factors,' I persisted. 'And I never see any Latvians.'

'You visit your mother,' Louise replied. 'In any case, what sort of cultural factors do you mean? I thought the Latvians came here after the Second World War. They might not regard themselves as fully assimilated, but it's not as though you're getting them fresh off the boat every day. Tell me two cultural factors about Latvians you'd have trouble with?'

'Their right-wing politics and their folk dancing.'

Louise laughed out loud.

'Pretend to agree with the first and pray they don't ask you to do the second.'

The secretary to whom I spoke when I phoned the New South Wales State Film Board seemed even more doubtful about my application for the job than I was myself. She told me finally, in the tone of one who has done all possible to prevent it, that I would have to see a Mr Basket.

'Ten-thirty on Wednesday, she said,' I reported to Louise, 'and then she also asked me to spell my surname three times. She told me that "Cavanagh" didn't sound like a Latvian name. I think she thinks I'm not authentic. Should I turn up in national dress to convince them?'

On Wednesday, at ten-thirty, I wished that I had.

Louise had done her best to prepare me. She'd spent hours every day firing words at me from Latvian and English dictionaries and timing how long it took me to give their equivalents. As a result I now knew the Latvian for many English words I never used, and was never likely to, and vice versa. In addition, I had memorised a great slab of bureaucratic prose (painstakingly supplied over the phone to me by a friend of Louise's) which described all the aims and functions of the State Film Board of New South Wales. I was now capable of fixing my eyes upon any interrogator and rattling off:

> *The State Film Board of New South Wales was established to promote and enhance the development of film in this State. The primary objectives of the Board are ...*

Here I could recite all the primary objectives from (i) to (vi), including the six subsections of primary objective (iv).

I repeated these to myself, over and over, in the bus on the way to the interview. It was one of those clear summer mornings which inspire Sydney people to suddenly tell strangers that they hate high humidity, as if this was some rare, strange obsession. There was a muted holiday atmosphere on the bus: children were chattering excitedly at inattentive parents and several passengers were holding neat packs of towels and lotions for a day's properly prepared leisure on the beach. The general air of anticipation cheered me. I began to think that maybe I *would* get the job.

But my good spirits were quickly deflated at the offices of the State Film Board where I sat for over an hour in a corridor, feeling both conspicuous and invisible.

The secretary who had been so doubtful of my application sat at a small distance from me, preoccupied with her finger-nails. Once I was seated, she never glanced at me, and none of the people who approached her desk seemed to notice me either.

Beside my chair was a door with a nameplate marked, very clearly, 'Bob Basnett'. It was like a reproach. The secretary had looked up at me irritably when I arrived. When I'd asked for Mr Basket, she had looked even more irritable.

'Take a seat. He's not in yet.'

I interpreted her glance towards Bob Basnett's door and her dismissal of me as an indication that I was to sit on the chair beside his door. So I had gone to it and begun my wait.

Too late, I realised there were other, more comfortable chairs in a corner across from the secretary's desk. It was one of *these* I had been meant to occupy. Instead I had managed to maroon myself on some spare piece of furniture that had been left ac-cidentally beside Bob Basnett's door. But I hesitated to move, paralysed by embarrassment even though it was clear from the looks of the people passing by, that they were surprised to see me there.

At first I assumed that Bob Basnett would be coming any minute, but time passed very slowly as I sat in agonised self-con-sciousness. I soon became convinced my wait was pointless. Someone else had been given the job and Bob Basnett had for-gotten to leave instructions about cancelling my interview. But still I was incapable of leaving my chair.

Instead I began to experience that sense of dream-like unre-ality you sometimes get on long train journeys, when you feel you've forgotten why you're travelling and you start to believe you will never arrive. I felt as though I could sit there, over-looked, for hours.

My equanimity was only restored when it occurred to me that sitting interminably in bureaucratic corridors had probably been a fate only too common for members of my mother's family. Then I remembered that my maternal forebears in Latvia had been rural folk. They probably had never lived close enough to any major centre to spend their time, ignored, in some Tsarist official's hall. But nonetheless I invented an ailing great-grandmother who was waiting in a chilly corridor. The reason: her eldest son has been conscripted. Eventually a clerk appears. 'Go back to your village, old woman,' he says to her, 'His Excellency will see no more petitioners today.'

I was re-running this story in Latvian as practice for the interview (if it ever took place) when a ginger-haired boy in overalls came hurtling by me. He was carrying reels of film and nearly hit me with one of these. He gave me an astonished look, then an apology as he went on rapidly down the corridor. I glanced after him. This was the first time since I'd arrived at the Film Board that I'd seen any indication that this was not just an office of another Government Department. Certainly there were some film posters on the walls, but I had been expecting more than this from a State Film Board and was unimpressed.

The red-headed technician didn't disappoint me though. As I watched, he raced the full length of the corridor and pushed wide open the door at the end of it. The door closed slowly enough for me to see a bright room filled with white cane lounges and palms: the glossy film world of my imagination. Afterwards, whenever anyone went down the corridor I always strained to catch a glimpse of this room. I called it the Promised Land.

Meanwhile my Latvian great-granny's plight was worsening. I imagined her going out into the snow. Her youngest boy was conscripted while the oldest died of cholera on the way to the Crimea.

An hour and a quarter after my arrival a tall dark-haired man approached the secretary's desk. She was busy with the switchboard, but managed to free a hansod and indicate an entry in an appointments diary to him with a remonstrating tap of a long scarlet fingernail. I saw him frown as he gazed at the empty visitors' chairs. Finally he noticed me. He turned back to the visitors' corner, gave me a second look in surprise and then was standing beside me murmuring something about a mix-up of appointments.

Bob Basnett was in his late thirties. He ushered me into his office with a minimum of words. We both sat down. He began to stare at the surface of his desk and then asked me where was I working at present? I said that I had just left university.

'You studied Latvian there?'

I explained that my mother was Latvian. I added, untruthfully, that we always spoke the language at home. Could I read it? I said yes.

This seemed to mark the limits of his ideas on how to run an interview because immediately after that he removed two closely printed pages from a file on his desk and asked if I could translate them into English.

I was glad of the activity. The pages seemed to be an excerpt from an interview with two people called Leblenis and Balodis. My throat was dry, but I started. The translation was difficult— not because of the language but because of the content. The interviewer's questions were easy to follow. Not so the replies.

Balodis and Leblenis answered in somewhat erratic alternation. Balodis usually gave short replies and Leblenis long ones, but many of Balodis's brief answers were so short as to sound elliptical: 'The camera,' he said on at least three occasions, 'shows the movement.' After each of these concise announcements (which never seemed to bear much relation to the questions he'd been asked) he sank into enigmatic silences. Leblenis sometimes amplified these terse replies, but never in any fashion that enlightened me. His responses were great long chunks of prose, very complex and—to me—nearly incomprehensible; but I still preferred them to Balodis's comments because I suspected that they were elevated nonsense—whereas with Balodis, I feared I might be missing the point.

I began to understand that Balodis was a film director and Leblenis his producer. They were discussing three films which were set in rural Latvia in the period between 1905 and the end of the First World War. I couldn't learn anything more specific about the films because Balodis, when asked, simply replied that the films were about 'the peculiar tragedy of the peasants'. He was very fond of that phrase and used it frequently, pretty well regardless of context. I was trying to think of some other way of phrasing it when Bob Basnett said, 'That will be enough, I think.'

I returned the pages to him and thought as I was doing so that the experience had probably been as uncomfortable for him as it had for me. So I said apologetically,

'I hope you could follow at least some of that.'

'You made a lot more of it than some of the others I've heard,' he answered. 'One of the other applicants said it was nonsense.'

Privately, I thought there was a lot to be said for this point of view, but I also knew I wasn't going to be the one to say it. I was realising that Mr Basnett thought I had done a passable job. I assumed he would now start enquiring about my translating experience. Instead he stood up. 'I think we'll go and see Stuart,' he said.

In the corridor, he asked whether I was familiar with Balodis's work.

I shook my head. He made no further comments until he opened the door at the end of the corridor, and said, 'Stuart Cullen is the Director of the State Film Board.'

I nodded, too startled to make any other response. Bob Basnett divulged information in a *sotto voce* way that made what was happening seem even more improbable. I really was in the Promised Land and here were all the trappings I had imagined:

lights, lounges, posters, luxuriant pot-plants. Mr Basnett indicated a seat, murmured that he would only be a moment, and disappeared.

Within minutes he returned, accompanied by a tall, bearded man who advanced towards me with rapid steps, smiling, his hand outstretched.

'You're Erika. I'm Stuart Cullen. We're very pleased that you were able to come in and see us.'

This was definitely going to be the charm segment of the morning's program. Now I was smiling back, shaking hands with Stuart Cullen, saying goodbye to Bob Basnett and being steered into the Director's office before I could think any further. Stuart Cullen meanwhile kept saying what an interesting project this was, such brilliant cinema, and—without a pause—introducing me to his secretary who'd just appeared, as if quite confident our paths would have crossed before:

'Erika—you know Ava? Ava Markham. Erika has come in to take a look at the Balodis films for us, Ava.'

Ava Markham smiled at me. She was in her fifties with a lined but striking face and hair which was severely pulled back. She asked if I would like coffee.

'And do bring us some of those nice French biscuits, Ava, the ones with chocolate. They're my favourites,' Stuart Cullen added to me with a smile. 'Now we must find you somewhere comfortable to sit.'

He glanced round the large, elegantly furnished office as if nothing in it could possibly be suitable. Finally he proffered a large white armchair.

'You've not had any—what's the best word for it—dealings with this organisation before, I take it?' he enquired.

I squeezed in a no before he continued, 'But I expect you're acquainted with us through the Film Festival?'

I could take a hint. 'Yes,' I said, 'I ...'

'You attended last year's?' he asked.

Ava Markham came in at that point with the coffee and the

special-request biscuits, saving me from an outright lie.

'Some films ...' I said, '*La Trahison des Clercs*,' I added, desperately trying to think of another film. I *had* seen *La Trahison des Clercs* but not until after the Festival when it was commercially released—and really I had only seen it because I'd liked the title. However, this sole example seemed sufficient because Stuart Cullen was nodding:

'Rouffiat,' he said. 'It's a new direction for him, of course. I wasn't sure that he would be able to make the transition successfully from those rather modishly *noir* works he's been making with Juliette Barry, but when you think of *Chloe dans Trouville* it's easy to realise that ...'

In fact it would never have been easy for me to realise whatever it was that came so easily to Stuart Cullen because I had never heard of *Chloe dans Trouville* before. But this was the least of my worries. Soon I would be having the greatest trouble keeping up with Stuart Cullen—for not only did he talk all the time in this rapid allusive fashion, but as he talked, he walked.

The walking wasn't aimless. Even as Stuart mentioned Rouffiat he fetched me a book from his shelves. *The Films of George Rouffiat*, its cover said. Then Stuart drew my attention to a print of a post-impressionist painting in reference to another point he had begun to make about the use of light in French cinema. Then he did a sweep past a film poster, tapped the spine of two books on Bresson, directed my gaze towards a still from a Hitchcock scenario, circled his desk, collected his cup of coffee and between sips described the camera work in two early Jean Negulesco films.

He was like the narrator of one of those television series on the History of Culture. Clearly my role was meant to be that of the home viewer: to sit, to watch, to listen and to discover. If I fell down somewhat in this I doubt he would have noticed. He was too busy telling me, at last, about Peteris Balodis.

This took much longer than you might expect because he incorporated into his talk a broad survey of world cinema, past and present. We approached Balodis via Melies, Lumière and quite a few of the names you'll find in the opening chapters of any standard film history. Then we proceeded through the Silents, the Talkies, the Rise of the Hollywood Hegemony, parallel developments in Western and Eastern Europe, the periods immediately pre- and postwar and nearly everything else until we finally reached Balodis as the next stop from Azerbaijan.

I almost missed our arrival.

Stuart was saying, 'We *have* been seeing films from the smaller republics of the USSR since about 1960. And, of course, we could have been seeing them long before that if we—and by "we" I don't mean only the Australian cinema-going public, but also that in Europe and North America—if we had not been so blinkered in our own cultural provincialism and so predisposed to the Hollywood formula. Yet, even today if you asked most culturally well-informed people for the name of a major film-making centre in the USSR outside Moscow, they would never mention Azerbaijan even though ...'

I didn't hear the end of the sentence. I was suddenly feeling inadequate as a culturally well-informed person, because I had never thought of Azerbaijan as a major film-making centre either and now it dawned on me that this was exactly the sort of thing that the State Film Board might expect its translators to know. On criteria like this, I'd fail. I felt depressed. The warmth of Stuart Cullen's welcome had given me the impression that quite possibly I was going to get the translator's job. With Azerbaijan I changed my mind. As Stuart Cullen talked and walked I found myself uselessly reviewing what I *did* know about the place—which was very little. Then I became aware that while I'd been recollecting all I knew about Azerbaijan, Stuart had been bringing Peteris Balodis, once again, into my sights.

'Balodis was born in Latvia.' I came so sharply to attention that I repeated this to myself. Balodis was born in Latvia. 'He grew up in Latvia.' I decided that I could absorb this without the need for repetition. I waited earnestly for more.

There wasn't a lot to come. Later I realised that this was practically all that anybody at the State Film Board actually knew about Peteris Balodis. Later I also realised that Stuart Cullen could span a great ignorance with a couple of generalisations and several detailed comparisons:

'Balodis,' he began again, 'seems to have had an unorthodox career for a Soviet film-maker. The name of his accustomed associate and producer, Andrievs Leblenis is, if not a familiar one, at least known. We hear of him at Mosfilm with Orlovsky and, for some time he worked with Melinov ...' Here Stuart digressed once more, this time onto the career of Melinov, who had lately encountered political difficulties with the Soviet authorities ... which brought him in a neat swerve back to Balodis again:

'This is what makes the achievement of Balodis so astonishing!' he exclaimed. 'How did this unknown Latvian film-maker who is clearly of peasant origin—the evidence is all there in his films—and who has, as far as we can establish, directed only one short documentary prior to this, how did he manage to obtain the backing and the autonomy to create these three brilliant films?'

Stuart Cullen paused briefly and dramatically after posing this question, and was even stationary for a moment.

'What makes it all the more mysterious and astonishing is that these three films are separate and independent narratives yet they were planned from the beginning as a trilogy; and that it was in this form, as a trilogy, that Leblenis and Balodis originally sought funding for them—and obtained it! I can think of no comparable situation in which two such unknown film-makers have received such massive Soviet support.'

This seemed to be only the beginning of all the mysteries and astonishments. The trilogy of films was made, Stuart informed me, but not in chronological order—and no-one seemed to know why. Balodis made the film called *The Daugava Line*, which was set during World War I, first; then he made a film which was set during the Revolution of 1905, called *Spring Days*. Finally he made the middle film, which was entitled *The Story of the Year of 1912 in the Village of Elza Darzins*.

Moreover, Stuart Cullen again informed me, although the films were made quickly in succession so as to be released as a trilogy, not one of them had ever been screened publicly.

I had rather more of a struggle to follow all this than the summary might suggest because Stuart included in his explanation several comments on Balodis's developing skill together with reflections upon the themes of Balodis's films and comparisons with the work of other Soviet film directors ... so that I spent half the time floundering in his wake, unsure whether the films he was discussing were those of Balodis, or of Tarkovsky or of Eisenstein or of several other great Russian directors whose names now escape me.

But while Stuart praised both *The Daugava Line* and *Spring Days*, it was obvious that his main interest was in Balodis's last-made and longest film. I repeated the title to myself: *The Story of the Year of 1912 in the Village of Elza Darzins*.

I liked it.

I had a history of liking film titles. It could be said that this was really my only qualification for the position at the State Film Board. I liked book titles too, but they never had the evocative power of film titles, and over the years I'd been attached to *Juliet of the Spirits*, *Closely Observed Trains*, *Deux ou Trois Choses que Je Sais d'Elle* and especially *La Guerre est Finie*. As you may remember my current favourite was *La Trahison des Clercs*.

I had barely finished contemplating *The Story of the Year of 1912 in the Village of Elza Darzins* when Stuart Cullen announced he was sure this film would soon be regarded as a masterpiece. He became quite excited as he spoke of it. He saw *The Daugava Line* and *Spring Days* primarily as warm-ups. *The Story of the Year of 1912 in the Village of Elza Darzins* was in another class altogether, a much more complex and personal film than either of its predecessors.

It was this film, however, that had caused all the trouble.

The Soviet authorities had condemned it as soon as they saw it. And as a consequence neither *The Daugava Line* nor *Spring Days* were released either.

'Moreover,' Stuart went on, 'as you may know, when works of art are censored in the USSR, not only are they never exhibited, there is no public reference to them. They disappear. It is as though they have never existed.'

I nodded, grave-faced. I understood what he meant. It was the only thing my mother had ever told me about Latvia under Russian rule. Once, when I was seven or so—and aware enough to notice that my mother's past was, somehow, never mentioned—I seated myself on a stool at the kitchen table while she was cooking and persisted in trying to elicit information about her as a little girl. She started doing what she always did, which was to say that it was a long time ago, that she'd been very young and that she could not remember. Then her mood altered—either I'd been irritating her or she felt, as parents sometimes do, a determination with children to be harshly realistic about the terrors of the world.

'Did you run away from Latvia because the Russians shot people?' I asked.

'They didn't shoot people,' she answered. 'They took them away.'

'Where to?'

'We didn't ask in case they took us away too. They took away whole families, mothers, children, babies, everybody. We just pretended that we didn't notice they were gone.'

'But where did they go to?' I persisted.

She answered: 'I don't know where they went. They were just taken away.'

Stuart Cullen, however, mistook my *reverie* for something else.

'You're probably wondering,' he said, 'in view of all this, how it came about that I was able to obtain these three films for screening at this year's Sydney Festival?'

The answer to this seemed to be: 'With difficulty.' Reports of the films had recently leaked out, and so when he was in Moscow the previous September he had decided to see if he could find out something about them.

'In the nature of an experiment really,' he explained. 'I wasn't expecting to learn much, but I was intending to be on vacation in Russia for several weeks and I knew that I would never have such an opportunity again.'

He described what had happened. His first tentative references. Feigned ignorance on the Soviet side. More direct feelers from him. Polite backings and shyings-away from them. Finally he began to ask direct questions and they told him outright lies.

'They sent me from one official to another. One said that the films had never been edited. Another told me that the only existing prints had been irretrievably damaged. Yet another one said that shooting had been cancelled halfway through on all three! But I kept on asking. I knew that I was being difficult. The last thing that the Soviet authorities want is to have some foreigner see a proscribed film and sing its praises abroad. Apart from all the implications that this has for their censorship, it also has exactly the same effect that praise from overseas critics has on our own Australian films: it makes the locals that much more interested. Nonetheless, I persisted.'

Stuart Cullen took a couple of steps towards me by way of emphasising his resilience.

'Fortunately,' he began again, 'I had one strong point in my favour. You see it's possible for the Soviet authorities to ban one obscure director's film without there being much reaction. It's easy enough for them to ban two, but it begins to look a bit odd when they ban three. The situation was an extremely sensitive one. Somewhere in the Soviet bureaucracy there were some very red faces and my enquiries were making life extraordinarily uncomfortable for these people. No bureaucracy is monolithic. With my questions, I was putting a sharp probe in the soft underbelly of the Soviet state.'

He paused for a moment, standing, facing me, his shoulders held proudly back. He looked like a victorious hunter posed before the trophy of his kill. He could have had the soft underbelly of the Soviet state pinned out on the wall behind him.

The hunt went on. He went in and out of offices, waited for phone calls that never came, pestered diplomats and any resident foreigners with influence for assistance, and finally began to see some success.

'When the Russians finally admitted that the films existed,' he explained to me, 'I knew I was making headway.'

I nodded. I was, I admit, becoming absorbed in his account. Again, later (but not much later) I would realise what a good politician Stuart Cullen was. Now in fact I found myself becoming increasingly sympathetic towards him. So when the suspense began to build up I found myself running with the story.

It was the night after the Soviet authorities finally told him he *could* look at the films, although they made it clear no subtitles in English would be available. He was in his hotel room and he had a wild idea. He rang the Australian embassy. He was told he was crazy. The embassy staff pointed out that he'd spent weeks grappling with the Soviet bureaucracy before they would even admit that the films existed. So, quite simply, they would never allow the films to be screened in Australia. It was a mad idea. The Soviets would be offended.

But, again, Stuart Cullen persisted. He pointed out to the embassy staff that the exclusive screening of these three films at the next Film Festival in Sydney would get round-the-world coverage. A first for Australia. The embassy then reluctantly agreed that they would support his request. The following day, after he'd looked at the films, he issued the invitation. The Soviet authorities were so taken aback that they didn't have the presence of mind to refuse his request immediately.

Then it was the last morning. He was standing at the window

of his hotel room, waiting for the phone call that would tell him whether his bold plan had failed or succeeded. I easily imagined myself standing next to him at that window. Below us in the wind-swept park, dun-coloured figures scurried and the birch trees swayed and dipped in the wind sending fans of yellow leaves out across the browning grass. I became as tense as he was. We both heard the phone ringing, and we both picked it up.

It was the official at Mosfilm. Saying yes.

Stuart Cullen stood there, wordlessly, by the side of his desk as though he was still in Moscow, at once disbelieving and delighted while he beamed at me.

Even so, final approval had come hedged with conditions. The normal procedure was to have the films subtitled in Europe, but this was vetoed. The films would be sent directly to Sydney in a diplomatic bag and be placed in the custody of the local Soviet consul. They were to be kept at the Soviet consulate at all times and could only be forwarded to the State Film Board upon a request in writing.

Then, when the films arrived in Sydney and were screened for the first time at the Board, another problem emerged. It was discovered that they were in Latvian.

'This too is unprecedented,' Stuart explained. 'For years the ethnic minorities of the United Soviet Socialist Republics have been complaining about the fact that their films, which have been made in their national languages, have been dubbed into Russian before being sent abroad. In this instance, however, I'm sure we were sent a Latvian-language print deliberately so as to increase our difficulties ...'

He smiled at me.

'And this, of course,' he added, 'is where you come in.

I looked up at him expectantly.

'I have given you a considerably fuller briefing on the background to this project than would normally be provided, because I want the successful applicant for this position to understand fully the importance, and the sensitivity, of the task for which he or she shall be responsible. This is not an ordinary translating assignment—this may well be an opportunity to participate in the making of cinema history. I can hardly emphasise too much the importance of the translator's role. Ideally—and I'll be frank, I'm looking only for the ideal translator; granted the immense demands of this project, it is only the ideal person that I shall employ. I cannot compromise—I want the translator who carries out this project to be not only highly skilled and to have a broad and appropriate range of experience, but also to have a wide cultural awareness and to be, if not completely sympathetic to Balodis's own political position, at least not ...'

'... not too right-wing.'

I could scarcely believe that I'd said it. Nor, it was clear, could Stuart Cullen. But now that I'd interrupted him I knew I had to keep on talking. If I let him continue with his list of qualities which he considered ideal, vital and indispensable to the person entrusted with the task—no, the mission—of translating Peteris Balodis's trilogy, I knew that I would be too terrified to speak up again. I kept the image of the birch trees blowing in the park in Moscow in my mind as I struggled to keep my voice steady.

'I haven't had extensive professional translating experience,' I said, 'but at present I am involved in translating an anthology of nineteenth-century Latvian poetry for a local publisher.'

I noted that I had been able to utter a whole sentence without being interrupted and that I still appeared to have his attention. Evidently he wanted me to say more about this putative project.

'All the poets are women,' I went on. 'They all wrote lyric poetry,' I added.

I was stumbling and I knew it. Given the silence with which this news was being greeted, I felt some conclusive statement was required.

'As you may know, Latvia was famous in the nineteenth century for its women lyric poets.'

I've always regarded this as one of the most improbable things I have ever said; but it came out sounding so authoritative that Stuart Cullen appeared to accept it as if the connection between nineteenth-century Latvia and women lyric poets was as well established as that between Shakespeare and Stratford-on-Avon. Later, I learnt that he accepted such inflated claims as a matter of course. All small countries and provincial centres believe that they have made some major contribution to art. The true scholar does not dispute these claims but understands why they arise and indeed considers them an indication of a healthy local cultural identity.

Unaware that my promotion of Latvia's women lyric poets was being viewed in this relativistic framework, I found Stuart's attitude very encouraging—I'd had many doubts the previous night when Louise and I had been devising the anthology. As usual, she had been very confident:

'Just rattle on,' she kept insisting. 'It *sounds* very impressive, and remember that none of them would know a Latvian woman lyric poet if they fell over one.'

I finished up by mentioning the names of some of the women poets.

Stuart began to nod approvingly. 'Perfect,' he said. 'Perfect, precisely the sort of background we need because, in addition to translating the films—where that sort of detailed textual experience will be invaluable—I have been given (this is absolutely confidential) copies of cassettes that Balodis made every evening as a sort of diary of his experiences while shooting the trilogy. Naturally we can't *publish* the transcripts of these cassettes, but we can circulate them discreetly to inform the critical reception of the films. In fact,' he went on, 'translating the cassettes will form the larger part of your duties. We expect to be employing you for quite a while, right up to when the Film Festival is held; and so what I propose is that you translate the first two films immediately, and then the cassettes and then *The Story of the Year of 1912 in the Village of Elza Darzins.*'

I nodded. The supreme task would be kept until last when I was fully equipped for it. Meanwhile, Stuart was talking and walking, musing first on the appropriateness of my experience ('The appreciation of nuance and structure that one obtains in the translating of poetry is certainly a valuable asset for our purposes ...') and then moving on to the expanding functions and structures of the State Film Board:

'I understand some of our critics have recently been saying that they don't know whether the Film Board should be more accurately described as an umbrella or as an octopus ...'

But I wasn't really listening. I was too busy being both delighted and excited, yet feeling at the same time a sense that this had been meant to happen. It had never been intended that I should be exiled to Gulargambone.

Gradually I became aware that Stuart Cullen was saying: '... although I'll be overseeing the project, I anticipate that I'll be away for varying periods of time in the next few months, so on a day-to-day basis you'll be reporting to Vince. I'll give him a call now and take you to meet him.'

Vince? While Stuart dialled the number I concentrated on recalling what he *had* been saying. Vince ... Marcus, wasn't it? The Senior Special Project Officer or Senior Officer in Special Projects or something similar?

'Not there,' said Stuart, displaying unexpected powers of concision as he put down the receiver. 'We'll arrange for Bob Basnett to introduce you tomorrow. Well, Erika, welcome to the Film Board of the State of New South Wales.'

CHAPTER 2

I should explain that all through the period of my life I'm describing, telephones rang constantly. In these days of pervasive technology and offices full of people quietly clicking keyboards, I feel that I'm exaggerating when I say that I spent a lot of time then waiting in someone's office for that someone to cease speaking into a telephone, even though I know it's true. My first day at the State Film Board was typical.

I sat and waited for nearly a quarter of an hour while Bob Basnett talked steadily into the telephone. Then he ushered me into Vince Marcus's office where there was a repeat of this performance—Vince too had the receiver jammed against his ear. He looked up as I entered, nodded at Bob's brief introduction from the door, then muttered 'LA' to me while pointing at a chair.

For several minutes I studied the desktop before me. Then I started to look around as Vince continued talking, unperturbed, completely absorbed with his telephone conversation. He spoke quickly. There were short pauses, interspersed with brief questions, terse comments, rapid double-checks. He put his head to one side so he could grip the phone between his neck and his shoulder while he made notes:

'No. No, Friday's no good. Saturday? He won't be there Saturday? Berlitz can make it Sunday. What was that number again? Three-eight-six ... only after midday local time. Has Berlitz seen Jack? He's keen ... he's talked to Forrest? Yes, that's what they told me too ... OK, I'll ring her right away. She said she's talked to Summers ...'

Berlitz, Forrest, Jack and Summers ... these, I felt, were only the beginning of a vast, unseen cast. Vince's office too was crowded: filing cabinets, all with papers spilling out from their drawers, occupied each corner while bookshelves and stacks of boxes formed barricades along the walls. Every surface was heaped with papers. A disconnected telephone, worn out no doubt by Berlitz and LA, sat precariously on a slanting pile of newspapers while its cord wound over a pile of boxes, disappeared into the melee for a time and then reappeared in a distant corner beside a bundle of folders stuffed with newspaper clippings. Crammed into the space between the chair in which I was sitting and the wall was a canvas chair with one of its back legs missing. It was now supported by several fat telephone books.

After I'd completed my survey of the room I gazed at Vince's dark head. It was gradually lowering itself almost to the desktop as he talked in rapid staccato to the mouthpiece, trying frantically to scribble some notes on a small white notepad. Suddenly the skinny red-headed young man I'd seen in the corridor on the day of the interview appeared at the door. He pushed his way into the office, added another couple of sheets to the mound in Vince's in-tray and was just leaving as Vince jerked upright and told the receiver to hold on before yelling:

'Kev! Hey Kev ...' His hand went across the mouthpiece. 'I'm all tied up here. Can you take this young lady ...' he pulled a piece of paper towards him and glanced at it '... Erika. Take Erika down and get the Balodis film going for her will you? It's the great bloody long one, with the crazy long title, *Elza's Story* or something. It's all ready to go. Thanks!'

A few minutes later I was seated alone in a small dark theatre while the opening scenes of *The Story of the Year of 1912 in the Village of Elza Darzins* began to unfurl before me.

Three hours and twenty-eight minutes later I stood up. Kevin was already rewinding the film in the projectionist's box as I passed. I called out my thanks and made my way slowly down the corridor again to Vince Marcus's office.

Ava, Stuart Cullen's secretary, was in the office with him. She was smoking a cigarette. He was dialling the phone.

'Here she is,' Vince said, disengaging his call. 'You see,' he added to Ava, 'I told you people survived it!'

Ava smiled at me and said hello.

Vince continued, 'Now she's going to tell us what it's all about.'

Ava ignored him. She told me she had an employment contract for me to complete and sign. She handed me the form.

'If you still want the job,' Vince interjected as Ava was leaving. 'Read the small print,' he directed.

'There's no small print,' Ava said from the door.

'No small print? What sort of half-arsed organisation is this?'

The phone rang as I was signing the form.

Vince put the phone down.

'Well,' he began, '*Elza Whatchacallit's Story* ... How was it? With the vocals? The sound all right? A bit fuzzy? It's a bit of an epic isn't it?'

I answered a general 'Yes' to all these questions.

'What'd you think of it then? Think you can do it? Any problems with the language?'

I took in a deep breath. 'Some of the minor roles are in dialect,' I said. 'Not completely. Just phrases here and there. I expect that was authentic for the period. In a village.'

This sounded to *me* as if I knew what I was talking about. I looked at him to see if *he* was suitably impressed. His face showed nothing. He was waiting for me to go on.

'Some of the main characters—Elza, and her father—they're a bit hard to follow here and there. The sound *is* a bit fuzzy. I'd have to see it again.'

'Sure,' Vince said, 'Sure. You'll see it again. Nobody expects you to sit down and write it all out for us straightaway.'

He continued: 'If this was all being done properly, we would've received a copy of the script complete with a glossary for any unusual terms or an annotated cassette of the soundtrack. But what we're going to have to do is prepare a cassette of the soundtrack ourselves. You'll do a transcript of that and then translate it. Bill King, the editor, will come and help you tidy it up into subtitles. To make it worse, as Stuart's probably told you, we can't even keep the films here, and the Soviet consul who's looking after them hates to let them out of his sight for more than a day. I think he thinks they'll defect or something. So, what's it all about anyway?'

I was afraid he'd ask that question.

'It's about the murder of the old man, Elza's father. He's the village schoolteacher. And who has committed it.' I'd begun hesitantly and I didn't feel that I was improving as I was going along—I was making the film sound too much like a conventional murder mystery. 'And the village's reaction to it—the murder.'

'Yes,' he said, 'That's—in part—what we thought. Sure.'

'Sure,' he said again when I didn't speak.

I was glad *he* was so sure. *I* really didn't have the slightest idea what the film was about. It was nothing like what I'd expected. Each time I thought I was beginning to understand it, it slipped away from me. I felt I'd spent the last several hours walking backwards, blindfold, through a dark swamp. On a black night. Faces and events and their relationships were all hopelessly scrambled in my memory. I could recall some specific scenes in their minutest detail, but I couldn't have made even the wildest guess as to what the whole was about. I finally said, helplessly:

'It's very good to look at.'

'Yes,' Vince said, 'He knows how to aim his camera.'

I didn't know if this remark was ironical or not.

'It's very complicated,' I added.

'Sure it is,' he agreed. 'It's those long northern winters. Gets them all complex and het-up.'

This all-too-simple explanation gave no comfort. Vince had issued the remark as if to pre-empt further irrelevancies. He sounded ... not impatient exactly, but as if he was attending to the matter mechanically. I felt that he wasn't interested, or—at best—that he was detached. His face looked faraway.

I was surprised and puzzled by his dismissive tone. In the wake of my interview with Stuart Cullen, I had assumed that everybody at the State Film Board held the name of Peteris Balodis in unremitting veneration. I was partly relieved by Vince's attitude (Stuart's enthusiasm had unnerved me slightly) but also taken aback. Was he being dismissive of Balodis's film just because he couldn't understand Latvian?

This seemed such an obvious injustice that I said, 'It must have been very difficult for him.'

'For whom?' Vince enquired vaguely. I had a feeling he was thinking of ringing someone.

'Balodis.'

He looked at me.

'Getting his films made in Russia—with all the bureaucracy and repression.'

Vince was still looking at me.

'Who told you that?'

I began to waver. 'Mr Cullen ... Stuart.'

Vince grinned. 'So Stuart has been spinning you a big fairy-tale has he?'

I stared back at him blankly.

'Balodis is good all right,' he said, 'but he's not only good, he's also lucky. He somehow managed to convince the Russians that he's the up-and-coming Eisenstein and when they wanted to throw some money around and encourage art amongst the masses in the Outer Parts, he (God help me if I know how) managed to have the greater part of the money land on him. The great undiscovered Latvian peasant film-maker! I'll bet he's no closer to being a peasant than you are ... Anyway, whatever happened, he was in the right place at the right time.'

'But they suppressed his work,' I objected. 'None of his films has been screened, or even mentioned publicly.'

Vince shrugged this away.

'I'm not surprised they were suppressed. That's not the point. What I want to know is how they got made in the first place. Films take time and people and money. Lots and lots of money. Roubles, roubles, roubles all the way. How did he ever get to finish them? Surely the Soviets must have been checking on him?'

He stopped and stared at me interrogatively. I shifted uncomfortably on my chair.

'Unlike you,' he continued, 'I didn't have a useful Mum who taught me Latvian, but there's one thing I can tell you and that is that *Elza's Story* is not a warm wonderful movie about valiant peasants gearing themselves up to overthrow their landlords and usher in the great revolutionary State. Balodis should have made a happy little movie about happy little peasants loyally loading happy tractors and trundling proudly off into the collectivised sunset. But instead he made *Elza's Story* where all the peasants start out bitter and twisted and get more bitter and twisted as the movie goes on.'

I couldn't tell if this was an accurate interpretation of the film or not but somehow I felt that he was missing the point.

'Perhaps that's what Balodis was trying to show?' I countered. 'What the Tsarist oppression was doing to the villagers.'

'Maybe,' he said, unconvinced. '*You* can follow what's being said, *I* can't. But I wouldn't try selling that line to the Soviet authorities. I mean, that the oppressed peasants can get so twisted from their sorrows that their Tsarist oppressors look like really nice folks in comparison. I'm not surprised they didn't appreciate Balodis's effort—I'm just astonished that he ever had the chance. How did he get away with it? That producer of his—Leblenis—must have had plenty of clout. I'd like to get hold of him. If he can pull off a deal like that in *Russia*, I could certainly use him *here*.'

I would have liked to ask him how he could use Leblenis, but there was another matter I wanted his opinion on.

'Why do you think they let us have the films?'

He looked at me as if he was getting weary of this topic. 'They probably got tired of Stuart talking at them.' He stretched in his chair and moved his hand across his face as if concealing a yawn and went on, 'Who knows? Sydney's probably a good place for them to make a fine display of being liberal. It's not New York or London or Paris. Hell, I don't know. Maybe they want to buy more wheat off us. In any case, it's a lovely deal for them. We can only screen the films twice at the Festival. And by the time they're up there on the screen, it will have cost us a lot of time and worry and money. So: two screenings, some glowing press coverage and then back home to Mother Russia. Bye bye, Balodis. Ava's fixed up an office for you down the hall,' he went on without a break, 'and she's arranging with the consul about getting the other two films for you to view tomorrow and we'll see you again then, OK?'

This was my dismissal. He was dialling the telephone with the end of his biro almost before I was on my feet.

As it happened, however, it was some time before I saw Balodis's first two films. The Soviet consul seemed to regard them as inherently dangerous materials, best kept locked up and never referred to, so the result was that the next day I spent most of the morning in a meeting with Stuart Cullen, Vince, Bob Basnett and Ava while they tried to work out a way of convincing the consul to release both *The Daugava Line* and *Spring Days*.

Then Stuart suggested that as preparation I should go and see all the subtitled foreign-language films that were screening in the city. Eager to be cooperative, I didn't tell him that I had already done this. Instead I went to see all the films several times more and to this day, I can impress people with my detailed knowledge of two mediocre French comedies, a bleak Turkish saga, a Spanish melodrama and a tedious Russian period film, which everyone else—including, possibly, the films' makers—has wisely and completely forgotten. This exercise didn't teach me much—except that subtitlers of films are a variable lot, and that the best films to subtitle are those with limited dialogue and lots of immediately comprehensible action.

Neither of which, I knew, would be true of Peteris Balodis's films.

The situation concerning their release was still unresolved when I returned to the Film Board two days later, but a compromise was being negotiated with the consul and in any case there had been a change of plan. Stuart Cullen proudly handed me a box containing several dozen cassettes—the tapes of Balodis's 'shooting diary', monologues of thoughts and reflections which he recorded every evening while filming the trilogy. I was to start translating these immediately.

I spent a great number of hours listening to these cassettes before I began the translation, and the more I listened the more mystified I became. Sometimes Balodis's comments were detailed and about events so minor that I was surprised he remembered them at the end of a busy day's directing. 'Slight cloud cover cleared by nine. Shirt of [the actor who played Elza's father] changed four times because of mud splatters ...' Sometimes his remarks were general: 'Feel that the pace of movement in this first half-hour must be slower than pace overall ...' But he never mentioned the actors' performances, scene rewrites or any of the things which I expected a director to be thinking about during a film shoot.

I increasingly began to wonder how Stuart Cullen was going to extract any critical insights from them. In fact I began to suspect that they might be no more than a therapeutic measure:

perhaps Balodis's doctor had suggested to him that he talk to the tape every evening as a means of winding down.

There were more than forty hours of tape to listen to. After twenty hours, a summons to the Director's office was a welcome relief. Stuart, I found, was uplifting as ever. He had not lost his sense of mission. He addressed himself to Bob Basnett, Vince, Ava and me with all the calm determination of a man who'd just laid a successful siege of Moscow:

'What we must do is persist,' he declared as he walked, 'and make it perfectly clear to them that we won't be swayed from our intention. You can be sure that all these problems are arising because the Soviet authorities are having doubts and no-one wants ...' (here Stuart Cullen took a decisive turn around his desk) '... this unpopular responsibility, so they're going to be obstructive. They're going to use every delaying tactic that they have at their disposal. But we ...' (here he advanced a few steps towards his four listeners) '... we have one great advantage which we shall exploit to our utmost ability: we know what we want and we are determined to get it.'

Braced by Stuart's oratory, first Bob Basnett, then Vince, then Ava, and finally myself, would all take turns and go and do battle over the phone with the consul and his staff, answering, again and again, the multitudinous questions: Who was to see the films and why? Who would collect the films and when? Who would sign for, and countersign for, the receipt and despatches of the films and who, in the event of the absence of any of these designated persons, would perform these tasks?

Eventually, success of a kind was achieved. Balodis's first two films weren't immediately forwarded, but instead we received cassettes of their soundtracks with a promise that the soundtrack of *Elza's Story* too would arrive shortly. It had never been proposed that the consul's office would arrange to have these cassettes made, but as Stuart pointed out during yet another meeting:

'This is a standard Moscow bureaucratic tactic: they don't

do what you ask them to do, instead they do something else which they claim is the equivalent. This allows them to retain the initiative ...'

He clearly intended to give instances illustrating this point, but Vince interrupted:

'Erika needs to see the *films* before she translates them. It's a waste of time translating from the soundtracks with no idea of the action.'

'It's not ideal,' Stuart agreed, 'but it is commonly done that way in Europe ...' He looked up at me expectantly.

I said that I would like to try. Privately, I told myself that listening to the soundtracks could not be any worse than listening to the tapes of Balodis's 'shooting diary'.

I was wrong—and Vince was right. Translating a film from its taped soundtrack without having seen the film was a slow and frustrating process. Whole conversations in Balodis's First World War film, *The Daugava Line*, were held against a background of cannon fire and the dialogue was often disjointed and hard to follow. I had to concentrate very closely, playing the tape slowly so as to catch every word.

As a consequence of this I became extremely sensitive to voices. I soon found that when anyone spoke in the corridor outside my door, my mind—like some rudimentary computer confused by overload—automatically began to register the conversation and to convert it into Latvian.

This was how I first heard about *At Half the Asking*.

Outside my door, a woman's voice declared, 'They're saying that *At Half the Asking* is too long.'

I was beginning to re-run this automatically in Latvian when I stopped. You can say at half the asking is too much. You can't say it's too *long*.

I rubbed my eyes and decided that life was getting like the tapes of Peteris Balodis's films. People were going around uttering the most peculiar, disjointed pronouncements. It was time for some coffee.

I went out into the corridor. Standing next to Ava was a woman who was not merely beautiful, she was striking. High cheekbones, silvery-blonde hair, large aquamarine eyes.

'Erika, this is Jacqueline Paley.'

Ava's voice jolted me back to reality. I realised I was staring. I said a hurried hello and raced off to the kitchen.

I had heard of Jacqueline Paley. Everyone at the Film Board was always talking about her. She was usually referred to in slightly hushed tones, as if she was some famed guerrilla leader come down from the hills to rouse the locals into insurrection. She was known for her virulent opposition to Stuart Cullen's policies.

Louise had explained it all to me. I was discovering that Louise knew quite a lot about the State Film Board and its employees. Her knowledge wasn't systematic, but had been collected haphazardly as a result of all her years of working in film and theatre. She knew, for example, that Stuart in his capacity as Director had a policy of hiring struggling film-makers like Jacqueline Paley and Vince Marcus in the hope that a period of regular employment might assist them in their careers. (Even at that time, this seemed to me to be a remarkably unwise even if well-intentioned policy, because artists are never grateful for being diverted from their work; I thought it went a long way to explain Vince's sardonic attitude towards Peteris Balodis. I also felt it accounted for Jacqueline Paley's opposition to Stuart Cullen.)

To my delight, Louise that evening was interested in talking about Jacqueline Paley.

'I'd forgotten she took a job at the Film Board,' Louise said. 'I expect she's broke. She's been trying to get a film going but there's always trouble with the money or the script. She's directed a few short films, but *At Half the Asking* will be her first feature. It nearly got going halfway through last year and I auditioned for the lead.'

'What happened?'

Louise grimaced: 'Jacquie didn't think I'd be suited to the part—she couldn't see me on a farm.'

As she was telling me this, Louise was curled up in an armchair, wearing black silk pyjamas and vivid red lipstick. Her long hair was pulled up on top of her head, held there by a clip of elaborate design featuring, amongst other things, the tip of a peacock's feather and two winglike formations in black satin. I thought that there was something to be said for Jacqueline Paley's point of view, but I shook my head sympathetically.

Louise had started work on a film which she disliked. It was based on a highly regarded novel set in Sydney during the First World War and was full of sensitivity, high ideals, painful and pointless loyalties and ineffable betrayals. Louise was bored.

'It's all good taste,' she had said, 'and nothing happens. All I do is walk slowly around gardens, twiddling my parasol, and smiling smiles of older-womanly wisdom while my young man talks at me about art and love. I don't know how I'm going to hide my relief when we get to the scene where I hear he's been killed at the front.'

I had grown very fond of Louise. Her need for an understanding listener at the end of a long day's frustrating work had achieved what her earlier 'encouragement' of me had never done. I had lost my self-consciousness around her. We were in alliance. I found myself collecting incidents and embroidering stories from my daily struggles with the works of Peteris Balodis to amuse her in the evenings.

Right now she was telling me about the story of *At Half the Asking*:

'It's from a script by Rita Clarke,' she explained. 'It's about a woman who leaves her husband and goes and settles on an isolated farm with her two kids and another kid who turns up. She has problems with the locals and floods and so forth and battles on. It's a great role for an actress. Especially for one of thirty-plus.'

I wasn't surprised by this plot outline. At that stage Rita Clarke had had three novels published and was generally regarded as the rising young novelist and star model for all aspiring women writers. I didn't like her books. My own view was that Rita Clarke had a fixation on women leaving their husbands and setting up new homes in isolated circumstances. If she didn't change her narrative soon, she would find that she had invented a whole new sub-genre: woman leaves successful husband and goes off with children to live in utterly new setting where she copes with local incomprehension-cum-hostility and finally comes to terms with both herself and her new environment. Rita Clarke's resolute lone mothers arriving with their offspring in unwelcoming neighbourhoods were becoming as familiar to me as nineteenth-century governesses alighting from carriages at country houses.

'Did Jacquie say what's happening about her film now?' Louise was asking.

I said no. I didn't explain that Ava had followed me into the kitchen and invited me to have coffee with her and Jacqueline, and that I had refused. This was partly from shyness, but mostly from embarrassment. I couldn't help feeling I was a fake.

I had discovered that in his announcement of my appointment, Stuart Cullen had given an effusive description of my translating experience. As a result, most of the staff of the State Film Board believed I was the leading local translator of Latvian women lyric poets. What's more, some of the staff believed I myself was a Latvian lyric poet. This had led to a number of awkward conversations in which kindly colleagues had struggled to say something appropriate about Latvian poetry.

Predictably Louise had been very amused, but *I* remained conscious that far from being a Latvian lyric poet on Australia's distant shore, I was in fact as *ersatz* a Latvian as it was possible to get.

I had told Bob Basnett that because of my mother we always spoke Latvian at home, but in reality the matter of my mother's country and language were so buried in my family that it was extraordinary that I spoke Latvian at all. My mother had arrived in Sydney as a Displaced Person soon after the Second World War and was given a job as a cleaner in a hospital. There she met my father. He had been a soldier and fought for several years without getting a scratch, but shortly after returning to his parents' farm he was thrown from a horse and was so badly injured he was sent to the city for treatment.

My father's family probably thought a Baltic refugee daughter-in-law was marginally better than a German or Japanese war bride. They dealt with the situation by never referring to it; and my mother must have soon realised that her own land and language were an embarrassment for my father and everyone connected with him in their small rural community. She never uttered a word of Latvian at home until I was four years old. This was when I discovered a box of Latvian books hidden deep inside our linen cupboard. Now I realise that my mother must have occasionally gone to those books when she was alone in the house and looked at them. She had lost everything else: her own family, country, language and past.

The sight of me leafing through the books and trying to decipher them must have moved her because she began to teach me a few words. I learnt very quickly and was eager to know more. Even then, I don't think I connected the language with her past: only much later did I do so. I was the sort of child who while growing up would probably have invented a private language if I hadn't had one at my disposal—and so for me Latvian became simply a fanciful, secretive and make-believe code. I began to learn it obsessively, valuing it only for its mysteriousness. I was so glad no-one else could speak it: around the farm I even forgot my mother could. All my games were now played in broken Latvian and soon I was talking to myself in Latvian all the time. It was a sort of private magic.

My mother stopped teaching me when I was twelve or so, but by then I was already fluent and I had become obsessed by the place itself. All the stories I invented were set in Latvia and I was constantly adapting its past, its present and its geography to fit in with my personal narratives. All through my teenage years I read everything that I could about the place. I spent hours in unvisited parts of libraries, gazing at small faded photographs of Latvia in old books and trying to visualise what the real country was like.

This phase of my life, however, finished abruptly when I was nineteen and had my first independent trip to Sydney, where I was to go to university. By then, things were changing. Australia had begun to admit the claims of its large postwar migrant population. Government programs extolled a mixture of cultures. Children of immigrant parents were being taught their parents' languages as a matter of course.

I was under a new dispensation too. My life was finally beginning. Although for a while I took out Latvian books—and even records—from the university library, these were no more than relics from my make-believe teenage past: soon I realised I had never been interested in Latvia as a real country at all. What I had wanted from Latvia was some sort of girlish romance: fir trees and snow and castles and other exotica that I never came across while growing up in rural New South Wales. And so these worthy academic books, with their uninspired covers and mostly undistinguished prose, their memories of Latvia's twenty years of equivocal independence and many centuries of bitter oppression, their standard pinings for their lost nation and its people and culture ... they did not connect with me. My own Latvia was, and had always been, a private country. It was largely imaginary. It had never had anything to do with what I felt about my own national allegiances—but it had everything to do with my right to create my own private world.

So while at twenty-three I felt that appropriating Latvia for my imagination and my diary was legitimate, being for the first time identified at the Film Board *as* a Latvian, and being paid for *being* one, made me feel guilty and inadequate. It seemed to me that the Film Board deserved a fitter representative of Latvia than someone who had spent most of her life inventing the place.

This discomfort was compounded by the fact that I was actually disappointed with my new job. I had imagined that it was going to make some great difference in my life but I was now aware that little had altered. Under these circumstances, I was pleased one morning to be intercepted by Vince as I was leaving the theatrette, having just sat through *The Daugava Line* and *Spring Days*.

'So,' he said, 'the Russians finally came across did they? Look—I'm expecting a call—come to my room and tell us what's been happening.'

He was gone before I could respond with anything more than a hello. He had been away all the previous week—the Film Board staff were always disappearing on trips interstate and overseas.

I had taken Vince's 'us' as an idiosyncrasy, but there *was* another man in his office. A large man with an odd-looking face.

Vince was on the phone. The other man rose to his feet. I wasn't sure whether this was in acknowledgement of my arrival or whether he was offering me his seat. He remained standing, hovering awkwardly around his chair. His awkwardness and large size, so noticeable in Vince's crammed office, made me feel unusually in charge of things. I gave him a smile plus a shake of my head, and with one fast efficient movement I scooped all the papers out of the canvas chair with the broken leg, placed them neatly on the floor and—without overbalancing the maimed chair on its uneven support of telephone directories—sat down. I was just about to introduce myself when Vince finished his phone call and said,

'Sorry about that. Erika, this is Greg Neath. Neath, Erika is our expert on Latvian poetry who is translating—'

The large man interrupted him. 'Is that safe?'

He was referring to the chair, though he didn't actually seem to be looking at it.

'Of course it's safe,' Vince replied.

'What happened to it?' the large man persisted. 'That leg looks as if it's been *chewed*.'

'It *has* been chewed,' Vince explained. 'It was my chair when I began to film my first feature. It's got my name on the back but I never had a chance to sit down in it: we had a horse on the set and it was tethered next to it and it chewed the leg off. I keep it for sentimental reasons. You want some coffee?'

While Vince was making the coffee I peered over the side at the chewed-off leg and then looked at the large man. I couldn't help staring at his face. Things sloped outwards at unexpected angles, or were too high, or too long or too wide. It seemed all misconstructed—but, fortunately, in an amiable rather than a frightening way, as though he was the village idiot from a very urbane village.

Returning with the coffee, Vince explained, 'Erika's translating those Latvian films which Stuart's finally gotten hold of. You know the man: Balodis. Anyway, we were expecting a tense-looking gent in a suit and white socks and we got Erika instead.'

I didn't know how to react to that introduction and neither, apparently, did Neath. He said nothing. Vince repeated his statement as a question.

'You know the man: Balodis? The great Latvian peasant film-maker suppressed by the Russians?'

Neath didn't seem eager to commit himself to that either.

'Perhaps.'

'We sent you a press release about him,' Vince continued. 'Don't you read our press releases?'

'Sometimes.' Neath had a mild, light voice.

'Sometimes!' exclaimed Vince. 'You come to all our screenings. You come to all our parties. You drink all our liquor. You sleep,' he paused 'through all our movies ... and sometimes, just *sometimes*, you read our press releases!'

Neath didn't seem abashed.

'It's been in all the papers,' Vince was adding. 'In fact ...' he stopped abruptly and began rummaging through a large bundle of papers on his desk, to finally extract a set of xeroxed press clippings about the Balodis films, '... here it is! In your own paper! In your own column! Don't you read that either?'

'I like to maintain my objectivity,' said Neath calmly. A smile slid across his face while his eyes seemed fixed in the middle distance. Belatedly, I realised that in addition to his mismatched features he had a marked squint.

Vince grunted. I hid my grin by sipping my coffee as he began to describe Stuart Cullen's pursuit of the Balodis films to Neath. 'Well, what do you think of all that?' he demanded as he finished.

Neath merely remarked that sex and nationalism always seemed to be causing trouble.

Vince looked frankly impatient with this broader perspective. 'Stuart has put half the Film Board's resources into winkling three films out of the Russians.'

Neath's eyes seemed to be stuck forever into the middle distance. Then one eye oriented itself in something like my direction and winked. 'It seems to have worked,' he observed.

Vince said angrily: 'If Stuart could put as much energy into local industry, there would be half-a-dozen more films in production in this state now!'

Neath smiled again. 'You've become a great localist for a director who's trying to get a project going in Hollywood,' he said. 'Why don't you tell me what's happening to *your* film?'

Vince grunted again. I was very entertained, watching Neath so competently deal with him. Vince decided to change the subject.

'They're still grinding on in there,' he declared, pointing to Bob Basnett's office. Then he added for my benefit: 'Jacquie

Paley's being interviewed regarding the funding application for her film—you've heard about it?'

I nodded.

'When she's through we're going out to have something to eat. Like to come?'

Neath joined in, 'Yes, come along. We don't know where we're going yet. Got any suggestions?'

I was about to answer when Jacqueline Paley herself walked in. She brushed her lips lightly over Neath's forehead, acknowledged me and leant over the desk to kiss Vince on the cheek.

'How'd it go?'

She shrugged. 'The males on the Committee don't like the male characters in the script,' she explained. 'Rita and I knew they wouldn't, but of course they didn't come right out and say so. They pussy-footed about and then finally the bravest one of them cleared his throat and said, Well, um, he wasn't sure that he found the male characters entirely believable and, well, um, he thought this was an important point because it's often said—though not by him, of course—that women can't create believable male characters. So I looked him straight in the eye and said in my most demure manner that perhaps that was because they felt that they didn't meet any believable male characters in real life ... Where are we eating?'

'Lucio's?' suggested Vince.

'I'm having dinner there tonight with Rita,' Jacqueline said.

'Paolo Sales,' announced Neath, 'says that you should never have dinner in an *Italian* restaurant. You may lunch in one, but you should always dine in a *French* restaurant.'

Jacqueline replied that she now had the best reason she'd ever heard for always having dinner in Italian restaurants: that way she would always be sure not to meet Paolo Sales.

'You've heard he's back with a film near ready to go?' Vince asked.

The other two nodded.

'Who's Paolo Sales?' I asked Vince.

'A bit of local colour that's been walkabout,' he answered. 'Well,' he continued, looking straight at me, 'are you coming?'

I said I was already booked for lunch.

Later on I regretted not accepting that invitation. Perhaps, if I had gone out to lunch with Vince and Neath and Jacqueline that day, everything might have turned out differently. But Jacqueline's brief hello to me had not been encouraging.

I had a sense too that they were all old friends. I didn't want to be on the edges, watching their shared lives and their shared familiarity. I was always feeling transient and marginal at the Film Board, and I suspected that this occasion would only make this worse. I was also very conscious that they were all at different stages of their lives and careers. My creative life, after all, consisted of only dreams and grand schemes plotted in Latvian in a diary while they were actually *living* theirs.

CHAPTER 3

Without any social life as a welcome distraction from the works of Peteris Balodis, after much effort and anxiety I was able to deliver the English typescript of the dialogue of *The Daugava Line* to Stuart Cullen. He glanced at it briefly, returned it carefully to its folder and remarked that we'd have to get the editor to have a look at it.

The editor was Bill King. He was wiry and very suntanned and had black sideburns with flints of grey in them that caught my eye every time I saw him. He was often at the Film Board editing and had come to see me several times—I'd grown to recognise his impending arrivals at my door because they were always heralded by sounds of greetings further down the corridor. Doors were opened, hellos exchanged, conversations started as Bill dropped in for a series of calls on my neighbours. Each time this occurred I was reminded of scenes in the comics of my childhood when the news of trouble in the jungle would be relayed from village to village until it finally reached the throne of the Phantom.

But the comparison ended there. Bill King's visits to me were always the briefest of his calls. He would stick his head around the door and say hello and ask how it was going. I'd say hello and all right. Then he'd say that's fine and we must get together soon but right now he was a bit pushed for time but soon, eh? And I'd say fine. Then he'd grin and shortly afterwards I'd hear him talking in the corridor, or else I'd pass someone's office and see him sitting there, drinking coffee.

After *The Daugava Line* I began work on *Spring Days*, the first (chronologically) of Balodis's trilogy. The film was set in the spring of 1905 when the Russian Revolution of that year was spreading from the cities into the countryside. It was very beautiful and full of omens and metaphors, but somewhat limited as to events. In my memory it lives as a succession of scenes in which the villagers are lined up on the bank of a river, gazing eastwards. Eastwards was the tumult of St Petersburg and Moscow.

Not much happened in Peteris Balodis's village during the Revolution of 1905 apart from a lot of gazing at the river. At the beginning of *Spring Days* the ice was breaking up: the first of the great logs felled in the forests upstream were coming down past the village, surging in the wild spring currents. The metaphor of the logs racing past the village wasn't lost upon me; nevertheless I found it difficult to understand why the wild spring currents would enthral the villagers scene after scene. I was often tempted to begin a sequence of subtitles with one of my own invention: 'Meanwhile, back at the creek ...'

I was also mystified because in those days before the fall of the Soviet Union, the 1905 Revolution was seen as Latvia's greatest moment in history. The Latvians had apparently revolted with such fervour that their version of the uprising—which swept through all the Tsar's dominions in that year—came to be regarded as a model revolution by Marxist historians and even conservative ones. Only in Latvia did the peasants join the uprising. Only in Latvia was there a major insurrection in the countryside. The peasants turned on their landlords and killed them in their mansions and then whipped the pastors in their churches for being allies of the landlords.

Yet, in Balodis's film, all the villagers ever did was burn down one landlord's house. And even this scene was ambiguous. The landlord's house wasn't a princely mansion. It was a pretty wooden house surrounded by blossoming fruit trees. As it was burning down, the locals stood about, looking rather taken aback by their one revolutionary act and very much as if they would have dashed to the flames with buckets if only someone had proposed it. Meanwhile the pastor died amiably in his bed and the landlord sailed equably on the Mediterranean.

I spent a lot of time wondering why Balodis had set a film about the 1905 Revolution in a village where nothing happened and how, furthermore, he had managed to get away with it. I never came up with an answer to the first question and as for the second, I could only assume that the Soviet film apparatchiki had been so taken by the beauty of the bucolic idyll screening before them that it was some time before they recollected it was supposed to be about the heroic events of 1905.

I didn't have to endure the frustrations of *Spring Days* for very long. One afternoon, halfway through the translation, I was summoned to Stuart Cullen's office.

Stuart was on the phone when I arrived, so it was Bob Basnett who began to tell me the news.

'There's some trouble about the Balodis films, Erika,' he explained. 'Apparently a local Baltic nationalist group has heard about the project and protested. A question was asked in Parliament this morning and as there's going to be an election soon ...'

He paused long enough for me to realise that the news was not good. 'The Minister is very concerned,' he continued. 'Spending on the arts is always controversial. This Baltic group claims that the Balodis films have been released by the Russians as Communist propaganda. So,' Bob Basnett looked at me sympathetically, then became businesslike, 'the Minister feels the only way to deal with this project now is to limit it. He's decided that only one of the Balodis films can be shown at the Film Festival. You are to stop all other work and start translating *Elza's Story* immediately.'

He averted his eyes, and it was this that stopped me asking the question foremost in my mind—if I did, I knew he would be obliged to tell me what I didn't want to hear. My job at the State

Film Board would now finish in a couple of weeks.

The silence was ended by Ava coming in with the afternoon papers, which bore headlines: 'Minister Attacked over Soviet Film Director' and 'Balts Call For Morris to Resign'. Stuart Cullen immediately terminated his phone call to glance at the reports. He rose to his feet and stood in front of Bob and me as if he were about to brief us for another special mission.

'I know that this situation looks very serious, but let me remind you that there've been a number of occasions during the last several months when the prospects for this project looked considerably graver than they do at the present juncture ...'

I don't recall much of his subsequent address, because I was completely preoccupied by a conviction that *I* was the cause of what was happening. And more than this, it was as though ever since I'd used my knowledge of my mother's language to semi-licitly get me this job, I had been waiting for these events to unfold.

Rationally, I knew that this was nonsense. The newspapers lying open on the desk before me told the story. The Minister for the Arts, the Right Honourable Sidney Everard Morris, was clearly in trouble. The Opposition had taken up the Latvian community's complaints in Parliament; and although they weren't interested in either Balodis or Latvian nationalism they were well aware how conservative voters would react when it was claimed that the Minister for the Arts had been using taxpayers' money to promote an obscure and—what was worse—Communist film-maker.

Yet I couldn't shake off that strange feeling of being personally responsible. As Stuart Cullen talked, my mind kept chasing down the threads of what I was experiencing as I tried to fathom whether it was a punishment or perhaps some projection of guilt, for what I had done. It wasn't hard to imagine that not just Latvia herself but also all her nineteenth-century women lyric poets had come back to haunt me in this way.

Now, looking back, I understand what it was. It wasn't a sense of crime and punishment, or guilt ... but recognition. With these newspaper reports I *was* rediscovering what I had first known as 'Latvia'. Balodis's films had never struck a chord because I had no clear visual image of the real country and its real people. While growing up I actually only knew about Latvia from newspapers. When I was twelve or so I discovered occasional items about my mother's country in the international sections of Australian newspapers. And this had led me to start looking through the press archive of the town library.

The newspaper collection had begun in the mid-twenties, a few years after Latvia and her neighbouring Baltic states of Estonia and Lithuania had become independent republics in the wake of the break-up of the Russian Empire at the end of the First World War. The articles were infrequent and were mostly introductory pieces about 'the little country and its people' who were usually described, in the capitalised sub-headings of the period, as 'Proud, Cheerful and Fond of Song'. In the 1930s, of course, times grew harsh. The articles then referred to Unemployment, Unrest and Instability as the economic crisis deepened and the build-up to the Second World War began. And by the start of the 1940s, Latvia had disappeared into the maelstrom.

In the newspapers, it became the road kill of history, a place that got invaded by armies marching elsewhere. The three Baltic countries proclaimed their neutrality, but were occupied by Russia following the Stalin–Hitler Pact. In 1941 Latvia went through 'The Year of Horror', when the occupying Soviet forces set out systematically to conquer the country by deporting all the most likely sources of opposition to the USSR. Thirty thousand disappeared.

When the Soviet forces retreated in the face of the German invasion, mass graves were found and some Latvians, like other Eastern Europeans, welcomed the Germans as liberators. But Latvia was only another unimportant country to be occupied by the Reich. This time the Jews died. When the German collapse began, the Red Army reoccupied Latvia, but by then thousands of Latvians were fleeing West and sometime later, a few of these appeared in the newspapers for me to see, not as blurred figures in refugee marches or as lines of faces in displaced person's camps, but as individuals, smiling at the camera, staring at a new country from the quayside: Latvians, like my mother, arriving in Australia as part of the great tide of postwar immigration.

Stuart Cullen's phone rang again and I noticed that Bob Basnett used that as an excuse to slip out. I was about to follow his example when Stuart signalled me to stay. On the phone he was telling a journalist that he was greatly saddened by what had happened, but that he thoroughly understood the attitudes of those members of the Baltic communities who objected to the screening of Balodis's films. In the rare gaps when the journalist was talking he would often look meaningfully at me, as if to say that only someone like myself who knew how much time and effort he had put into trying to obtain the Balodis films for exhibition could really understand how disappointed he *was* feeling.

But for one so disappointed he seemed surprisingly buoyant. He clearly enjoyed talking to the press and it was apparent he was very good at it. Moreover, I could recall from my first meeting with him that he had never really been interested in Balodis's two shorter films. From his point of view, therefore, the compromise that had been reached was really quite satisfactory. For *me*, though, things were far less comfortable. As Stuart Cullen talked away on the phone, memories rose before me of the hot worried mornings of summer spent reading the employment notices.

'Well, Erika,' he said to me, putting the receiver down, 'I think that what we do now is resolve to live to fight another day. Let's rally the troops. Vince Marcus is over at the Minister's office helping with any enquiries they get. Could you ask Ava to call him please, and get him to join us down at the local bar? Ask her to invite the rest of the staff and I'll call Greg Neath and a few of our other supporters and sympathisers.'

On the way to the bar Stuart informed me of his immediate plans. 'We have made this undertaking to the Minister, Erika,' he said, 'that all work on the Balodis project will be stopped except for that involved in translating *Elza's Story*. However, there will inevitably be delays with technical matters and we will require you to be in a position to oversee the process right until the very final phase when we have as perfect a subtitled print of *Elza's Story* as it is possible, within the scope of our considerable combined abilities, to achieve ... I am sure there is no need to emphasise to you that, especially after this latest setback, we bear an immense responsibility both to Balodis and to the cinema itself to fully utilise every opportunity available to us to present this great film in the most satisfactory context possible—this will mean that at later stages of the project, while technical matters are underway, you will undoubtedly have periods of unallocated time, and I believe these periods could be usefully directed towards continuing the translation of Balodis's shooting diary. I am sure that it will be possible for a considerable amount of the work to be completed.'

Although I wasn't exactly elated about the prospect of returning to Balodis's shooting diary, this did sound as if I had a reprieve. I suppose that I'd learnt a great deal about Stuart Cullen by this time because I don't remember having any difficulty understanding precisely what his words meant. The Film Board would comply with the Minister's instructions, but once the hue-and-cry had died down he would probably attempt to restore Balodis's first two films to the Festival program. My immediate concern was to find out what this meant in terms of me and my livelihood.

'How long a period of time do you consider we would be looking at?' I enquired. Stuart Cullen's circumlocution was quite contagious on occasions.

'Oh—a minimum of six weeks—to begin with,' he replied.

His polite dismissive tone indicated that this was an arbitrary estimate, plucked from the air, and that he might as easily have said four weeks or eight or ten.

I felt a tentative joy. Facing unemployment in a possible six weeks was considerably better than facing it in a probable two. My spirits were rising as I walked into the bar where I found I was, in a mild sort of way, the centre of attention. All the Film Board staff came up to me to express their sympathies on the cutting back of the Latvian films. I became so preoccupied receiving these attentions that I didn't notice Louise's presence. I only became aware of her when she thrust her hand, bearing a glass of champagne, through my little throng of supporters.

She explained that she had run into Neath who had told her the whole story. She had then accompanied Neath and Jacqueline and several other Film Board staff to the bar. Most of them now were listening to Vince's account of his day in the Minister's office.

'Your kinsfolk, Erika,' he said, starting his tale at the beginning again for my benefit, 'are a devious bunch. They cooked up this plan to have lots and lots of Baltic persons lined up outside the Festival cinema on opening night. All of them would be wearing ethnic dress and singing ethnic songs to purportedly honour Balodis and Baltic cinema and Australo–Latvian links. But then, when Eisteddfod Sid stepped out of his limousine and beamed at them they were going to turn mean and wave placards calling for his head for supporting a godless Soviet stooge-person film-maker.'

He stopped because we were all laughing. The Minister, 'Eisteddfod Sid', was famous for gracing as many public occasions as possible. In his own rural electorate, it was said that you couldn't christen a puppy without him wishing to officiate. 'Sid was terribly upset,' Vince went on. 'At first he took it all personally—kept on insisting that he'd never had anything to do with any of these Baltic people and that there weren't any in his electorate. Then the implications began to sink in and he started to realise how it might *look* to his local electorate—apparently he only got in with a very narrow majority last time. So he's very sensitive about his image. At one stage it looked as though he was prepared to burn Balodis at the stake if he thought that this might please the Balts.'

Amidst the general hilarity Vince described the proposals that the Minister's own beleaguered staff had thrown about in an attempt to mollify the Latvian community:

'... a series of heart-warming movies about the wonderful contributions that all the wonderful Latvians and Estonians and Lithuanians have made to their wonderful new country while still keeping vibrant and alive all those traditions from their marvellous old countries. The violins were roaring. We don't have to worry about getting work now, Jacquie. Soon we'll be directing sagas about Balts who came here with nothing but the shirts on their backs, and who worked twelve hours a day building the Snowy River irrigation system while learning English at night and upgrading their qualifications in any spare minutes they had left—'

'And it's about time too,' interrupted Ava firmly. 'I don't think the contributions that postwar migrants made to Australia have ever been properly recognised.'

I had a feeling Ava was saying this partly to remind Vince that I was present. He did give me a quick look before Jacqueline announced: 'It's McCarthyism, it's like America during the Cold War all over again!'

Everyone looked at her.

'Why did Cullen buckle like that?' she demanded. 'He's like one of those 1950s American liberals running for cover at the first sign of trouble. All talk and no—'

'I don't think,' Neath interposed, 'that this is true of either Stuart or of the American liberals—'

Jacqueline cut him off. 'You're always so keen on details,' she said. 'You spend your time trying to be fair and just and you're always waiting to see if everything can be proved beyond

doubt and counter-signed by three witnesses. You'd be in a cat-
tle truck on your way to a concentration camp and be claiming
it's probably just a re-routing of the normal service. Okay, so I
don't know every footnote. It all happened before I was born.
But I know what went on both here and in America during the
Cold War. And it's going to be like that again unless people start
speaking out.'

She had paused for breath, and now she was gesturing across
the room.

'... Look at Cullen over there. Usually you can't shut him up.
Give him the opportunity to talk on TV or radio about censorship and the right to free speech and he'll go on for weeks. But
he gave in without a fight. He didn't say a word about censorship at all. You know how he persuaded Eisteddfod Sid to let
us screen at least one Balodis film? He told him the Russians
would be offended if all three were withdrawn, that's how. He
could have pointed out that this crackpot Latvian group haven't
even seen Balodis's films—that they're just using them as an excuse to get public attention. But he doesn't even attempt a fight!'

There was dead silence. Then Vince said, 'I think Stuart did
the best he could under the circumstances, Jacquie. He used
the only argument Morris would listen to. Morris was all for
cancelling all the films this morning.'

Neath supported this. 'You know how mad Morris is. He
wouldn't hesitate to cut the Film Board completely if he thought
there'd be any votes in it. Stuart's fighting from a very weak
position.'

'And he's making it weaker by the way he's fighting,' retorted
Jacqueline. 'If he thinks Morris is mad, why didn't he approach
somebody else in the Government and try and influence Morris
that way? He's always hanging around with important people
and letting you know he can be discreetly influential. For all
his grandstanding, there's not much difference between him
and those Soviet bureaucrats who censored Balodis in the first
place.'

'Well,' said Neath in the wake of this new onslaught, 'that's certainly firing on your man from all sides.'

No-one else spoke. We were all aware that the object of Jacqueline's attack was just across the room. These were the sorts of circumstances in which criticisms were usually delivered by a sideways mutter or an innuendo, but there was nothing covert about Jacqueline's declarations. I stared at her, impressed but perplexed.

On one hand I felt Jacqueline was right: Stuart Cullen *was* an opportunist. But on the other hand I wondered how she'd react if she saw *Spring Days* with its minimalist agrarian revolution. I rather suspected she would come out in favour of the Russians for banning it. But all these were side issues. What impressed me most was her firm opinion of the subject. *I* was changing my mind every couple of minutes. It occurred to me that I should have been more sympathetic to the ineffectual villagers in *Spring Days* who found it so difficult to be whole-hearted and ruthless in their attempt at revolution.

It was Louise who broke the silence.

'What does this mean about your job?' she asked.

Trying to sound buoyant, I explained that I probably had another six weeks' work.

'Never mind,' she said, 'I got my next job today. Lead in a feature.'

I was delighted for her. 'How *wonderful*.'

'Yes,' she said, 'that's how I came to run into Neath. I was leaving Paolo Sales's office where I'd been signing the contract.'

This, it seemed to me, was a rather roundabout way of delivering this important news. Louise wasn't usually coy. I soon realised why.

Jacqueline was staring at her. 'You can't be serious!' she exclaimed.

Louise nodded.

'You've taken a job with that small-time con man!'

Louise observed that he might be a con man but he was no

longer small-time.

Jacqueline raised her eyebrows. 'And there's no strings attached? No you-be-nice-to-your-producer-and-your-producer-will-be-nice-to-you?'

Louise laughed. 'He's working so hard at being subtle that it's beginning to run and drip over the edges. All he ever talks about is how he has at least two other pictures in the pipeline and how these two in-the-pipeline pictures are going to be quality productions, and how he'd really like to build up an ensemble of good actors and how important it is that we start developing good roles for women over thirty because such a lot of our audience is in that age group now. Eventually he'll have me thinking that it's my duty to the Australian film industry to go to bed with him.'

If Louise had hoped that her wry account of Paolo Sales might deflect Jacqueline's indignation, she was immediately disillusioned. Jacqueline burst out, 'I would have thought it was the duty of any *good* actor towards the Australian film industry to refuse to appear in one of Paolo Sales's films.'

Louise didn't reply; and someone else changed the topic. But I felt angry on her behalf. When the others were out of earshot, I said, 'Jacqueline certainly takes a high moral stand. Doesn't she realise that people have to earn a living?'

'Oh, she's always like that,' Louise answered equably, 'I should have lined Neath up in advance to break it to her gently.'

It seems to me now that it was typical of Louise to regard moral outrage as being rather like wet weather—one of those things about which it's always wise to take precautions. But at the time I was too busy reacting to the implication of her last remark. I should have realised that morning in Vince's office that Neath and Jacqueline were lovers. Now, once again, I became aware I was amongst a group of people about whom I knew very little.

This increased my sense of outrage on behalf of Louise. I kept feeling that Jacqueline had been very unfair to her, and my resentment was fuelled by the knowledge that if Jacqueline was aware of how ambivalent I felt about working on the Balodis film then she would immediately say that in all integrity I should resign. My mind kept running through her arguments. It was *not* a matter of censorship. It was true that the Latvian community had not seen Balodis's films, but it wouldn't affect the issue if they had. What the Latvian group was objecting to was not the films themselves—but the fact that for propaganda reasons Balodis was now being supported by the Soviet Government in Moscow. If you accepted that Latvia was an occupied country, it followed that you would consider an artist sponsored by the occupying power as a collaborationist. And while the occupation of Latvia had happened so long ago that any links between it and the screening of three films in Sydney decades later might seem tenuous to a person who didn't know the background, I *did* know the background. Then I also remembered Jacqueline declaring, 'So I don't know every footnote. It all happened before I was born.' I could never have been as vague about dates as she was. She had no sense of history. It had *not* all happened before she was born—she was several years older than I was; and I was a Cold War baby.

'Are you leaving?'

I became aware that I was standing on my own, holding an empty glass. Vince was waiting for me to speak and when I didn't, he began again, 'I didn't mean ...'

He stopped. I waited for him to go on, but he just stood looking at me. It occurred to me that he might be half-drunk and I felt irritated. It had been a very long day and I'd had an oversupply of unexpected attentions.

He took a swig of beer and continued, 'I didn't mean to offend you about the demonstration. I must have sounded flippant, but that wasn't because of the Latvians. It was because of dealing with Eisteddfod Sid and his staff and watching the politics of it all.'

I said that I hadn't been offended.

'It's all bloody pointless anyway.'

I didn't know what he was referring to and kept silent. 'Morris, the Minister,' he began to explain, 'Morris wouldn't know the difference between a good film and the Wangaratta pig show.'

This sweeping comment didn't leave much scope for a reply, so I just nodded. I was familiar with the business of a man explaining the operations of the world to a woman. I looked up at him to encourage him to keep talking, but instead he started looking about the room in a preoccupied fashion. I said goodnight and went to say my farewells to Louise who was, inevitably, going out to dinner with some admirer.

In the bus on my way home, I felt lonely. There would be nobody with whom I could discuss the day's events.

As I recorded what had happened in my diary, my eyes began to get wet and I had to reprimand myself. I really didn't have much to complain about. With any luck my job might spin out a while longer—everyone had been sympathetic and had made much of me.

I should be grateful, not teary, I told my diary. My brief period as a heroine at the Film Board had gone to my head.

CHAPTER 4

My time as a heroine was certainly brief. The next morning at the Film Board, the only reference I heard to the previous day's events was a remark by Ava that Bob Basnett was replacing Stuart Cullen on an overseas trip—the latter was concerned there might be further trouble with the Balodis films and so didn't wish to leave the country. Otherwise, the matter seemed completely forgotten. I knew I shouldn't be surprised at this. Crises were frequent at the Film Board and I couldn't expect my own period of importance to last long, but the fact that it had lasted only one day reminded me that I was temporary and marginal to the place.

That morning, I examined every entry in the Positions Vacant pages of the newspaper columns. Then I counted all the change in my purse and planned economies, carrying out elaborate calculations in the newspaper margins.

All of this was partly to postpone the work at hand. I now found translating very tedious and it took a considerable amount of resolution merely to remove the cassette of the soundtrack of *Spring Days* from the player and insert that of *The Story of the Year of 1912 in the Village of Elza Darzins*. How glamorous and exciting it had all sounded the first time I had heard the title. Everything had seemed promising that day, but the promise had remained unfulfilled. I had some money and was very fluent in Latvian (for all the good that would ever do me) but my future was no more secure. My mood, as I set about the translation of *Elza's Story*, was grim.

So was the mood of *Elza's Story*. This was probably the only thing I understood about it that first day. *Elza's Story* was far removed from the vivid scenery and slow bucolic charm of the village in *Spring Days*. The year of 1912 didn't have the excitement and optimism of the revolution of 1905. In fact if anything, 1912 seemed to be a year of reaction.

The film began with a number of meetings of the village committee being set up to organise the following year's local celebrations in honour of the four-hundredth anniversary of the accession of the Romanovs. These meetings were central to the action of the film—or, at least I *thought* they were when I first began translating.

Within a few days I was doubtful of everything to do with *Elza's Story*. Of course I had known before I even started listening to the soundtrack that the film was complicated, but I soon found that it was even more complicated than I'd remembered from that initial screening. There were long sections that I had forgotten completely. Nonetheless I was immensely grateful for that one first, inadequate viewing. Without it I would never have been able, from the soundtrack alone, to understand the start of the film—when the various aged survivors in the village talked of their pasts.

As it was, I found I was working much more slowly than I had on either of the other two films. It didn't take long for the film's sheer complexity to unnerve me. After one particularly difficult day, I arrived home looking so harassed that Louise immediately asked if I was feeling ill.

'It's that film,' I said, sinking heavily into a chair. 'It's terrible. I just discovered today that three of the six survivors—the six old people who start the film by narrating their memories in 1950—well, three of them are actually dead. One of them gets executed in 1912 and the other two die in the First World War, and the characters whom you see talking are Elza's constructions of what she thinks these three people might have been like if they had survived.'

Louise had risen to get herself a drink. She turned then and looked at me thoughtfully and said, 'It's a murder case, isn't it?'

This made the film sound unduly forensic, but it was true.

It *was* a case of murder—that of Elza's father, the old school-teacher, in 1912—but what I couldn't understand about the six survivors (both the real and the reconstructed ones) was why, in their aged ramblings, they were so obsessed by this one incident. There had been so many deaths in the intervening years from wars, revolutions, invasions, deportations, massacres and assassinations, as well as from disease, hunger and cold ... yet the survivors kept on returning to this one long-gone death. Their aged voices were hard to follow on the cassette. I kept telling myself that surely things would improve when I got back to 1912 in the main part of the film.

However, the events of 1912 were even more difficult to decipher than the characters' confused recollections. There was more action in this section of the film, but it only served to increase my problems: scenes on the soundtrack faded out very quickly, taking with them significant chunks of dialogue. Elza, the heroine, had a number of long voice-overs which sometimes drowned out other conversations. Things always seemed to be getting lost: names, answers to questions, ends of sentences. I was constantly having to backtrack, replaying the cassette slowly, cutting it off at one-word intervals because I had discovered that my translation of an earlier section didn't connect with some later conversation. I began to spend increasing amounts of time writing down all possible meanings of a statement before making a decision about its content. I also took to repeating the dialogue aloud, emphasising it this way and that in an attempt to fully understand what was being said.

None of this was much use. The problem wasn't my knowledge of the language and my grasp of idiom. It was that the dialogue itself was very dense and obscure. I was prepared to accept this from Elza, who regarded herself as the community's resident intellectual and often spoke in arcane fashion. But I considered it a bit odd in the rest of the villagers. Balodis's rural folk from Latvia seemed able to squeeze into their conversations more ironies and ambiguities than I would ever have imagined possible. As I told Vince Marcus one day, I was beginning to be relieved that my mother had been obliged to get out of the place.

He had come into my office and had found me deep in one of Elza's many monologues. I was saying it aloud, word for word.

'Are you translating that or memorising it?'

'Sometimes what they're saying doesn't quite ... jell,' I explained. 'It's easier to follow if you say it out aloud. Even the ordinary villagers seem to talk to each other in the most obscure and elliptical manner.'

He came over to the desk and stared at the cassette. 'Is there a lot of dubbing in it?' he asked.

I was too preoccupied with a question of my own to answer him. Only later did I realise how relevant his query had been.

'When Stuart saw the film in Moscow,' I asked, 'how did he follow it? Did they do a translation for him?'

Vince explained that Stuart Cullen had probably been given a brief outline in advance, while a running translation had been made during the screening by an interpreter working from a dubbed Russian print.

'Oh,' I said. I couldn't envisage how anyone could have even understood the action of *Elza's Story* when it was communicated by these means, much less decided that the film was a masterpiece.

Vince merely smiled, as if I had much to learn about the practice of film festival directors. 'Talking of travelling,' he stated, 'I'm going to LA tomorrow.'

He had never discussed his movements with me before. On this occasion, however, with Bob Basnett away I supposed he thought it appropriate to tell me what was happening. His manner, however, seemed more friendly than supervisory. I asked why he was going to LA.

'I'm going to grovel to a mogul.'

'You mean Berlitz, Forrest, Summers and Jack?'

He seemed a bit taken aback but said, 'Summers is actually the mogul. But I guess I'll have to do some grovelling to the others too.'

I would have liked to ask him more, but he was ready to leave and said, 'Perhaps you'd better see that film again if it's really worrying you.'

When he was gone I contemplated the work before me despairingly. I hadn't wanted to tell him, but I had preempted his advice. I had already seen *Elza's Story* for a second time—and it hadn't made any difference. After the first screening I'd told Vince himself that it was about the murder of the old schoolteacher and the villagers' reaction to the murder; now, after days of work and worrying, I knew that I couldn't improve on that bare-bones summary. I *still* could not understand *Elza's Story*.

I did understand that the murder of the old schoolteacher was of great significance: as a supporter of Russian rule, he was suspected by the villagers of reporting on them to the Tsarist police. Therefore the villagers had hated him and welcomed his death—until they learned of the Government's intention to consider his murder as a political matter. As a schoolteacher, Elza's father was a State employee; thus his murder could be treated as an official assassination. The villagers maintained that every resident had an alibi and that the crime must have been committed by a passing tramp. But there were a number of suspects, of whom the most likely was Elza's Jewish lover, Alexis. The villagers hated Alexis almost as much as they hated Elza's father, partly because of their rampant anti-Semitism, but mostly because Alexis was such a suspicious and unlikeable character. As such he was the perfect scapegoat.

Yet the villagers never denounced him. Even when the Tsarist soldiers arrived to conduct their last brutal interrogation and the villagers could have used Alexis to save themselves, they did not incriminate him.

This was perplexing, to say the least. The only reason I could find to account for it was a quarter-minute conversation in which one villager said to another, apropos of nothing in particular, 'Alexis did not kill the teacher.'

'No,' replied the other villager, 'he did not.'

Neither speaker gave any reasons for this conclusion and neither referred to it afterwards. Yet immediately following this conversation there was a scene in which Alexis, looking grim-faced and watchful, moved through a low-skied evening to the isolated schoolhouse where you knew the old schoolteacher was alone. The next shot was that of his body, hunched up in the shadows by the wall of the schoolroom.

There were times when I even wondered if the murder had happened at all. Various significant scenes were reconstructions from people's memories and the presentation was so ambiguous as to sometimes suggest that perhaps the whole drama had taken place in a dream-life in which all the village shared. However, if this was the case, it seemed to be the only thing they *did* share. As a community, they were certainly vague about detail. I was beginning to notice that they often confused names and events and contradicted themselves.

Some of this inaccuracy, of course, was a function of the plot: people were lying to protect themselves, and so they fabricated alibis which negated those of their neighbour. But this couldn't explain why sometimes characters would say one thing one day and the opposite the next. It was as if their powers of recall couldn't hold out for twenty-four hours; on several occasions a speaker would muddle the names of his own closest relatives and neighbours as if he had just arrived at a party and met too many people to recall the introductions. At first I thought that these discrepancies were due to my inexperience as a translator, but I spent so many hours assiduously checking and double-checking the cassettes that eventually I had to conclude I was only translating what I was hearing. All the discrepancies were, in fact, intrinsic to the soundtrack.

I then decided that it was all deliberate. Doubts were being cast upon the memories of the survivors. The audience was being warned to be suspicious. But I couldn't see any reason for this, and the whole basis of the film was the importance to the survivors of this one killing that had happened nearly half a century before. It was therefore vital that they could all recall this one event from their past as though it was yesterday.

Elza herself was a major problem in this regard. She narrated the film, introducing each section with a few statements. But often she didn't limit herself to preambles. Her voice-overs ran through complete scenes so that frequently it was nearly impossible to hear parts of the conversations between the villagers themselves. And of course a conversation was always occurring. It became clear to me that whatever else happened in Balodis's Latvia in 1912, people talked a great deal. None of my preconceptions of grim silent peasants, given to long periods of brooding, applied in his community. I was barely a quarter of the way through the script when I began to think that the 'peculiar tragedy of the peasants' to which Balodis had so frequently referred in his interview was that they'd been born a century too early for talk-back radio. In my frustration I could easily imagine all the residents of Elza Darzins' village getting on the phone, impatient to be on the airwaves, eager to tell all the listeners out there what had really happened the night that Elza Darzins' father was murdered.

Elza was very much at home in this hyper-talkative community. She, in fact, was the film's culmination, its highest point of loquacity. She rarely stopped talking. At first she stuck to recounting events and setting the scene, but as the film went on, she began to talk at much greater length and on a wider range of topics. She philosophised about life, threw in a few sibylline remarks about events underway and, now and then, provided bits of irrelevant sociological data about minor characters whom you rarely saw. She seemed to me to be a mixture of the authorial voice, a one-person Greek chorus, a budding Marxist finding illustrations of the class struggle in local life, and an anthropologist with a bent towards tragic poetry reporting on a case study. But most of all—like the other villagers—she too was unreliable.

I first became aware of this when she announced to the audience that Alexis had tried to persuade her to run away with him 'at the time of the harvest when my father died'. This was news to me as I knew her father's murder had happened months before the harvest, during the planting in fact. I backtracked the cassette and confirmed that I was right. Then I checked every Latvian dictionary I could find and concluded that, as you might expect, the language distinguished very clearly between a planting and a harvest. I was puzzled. Obviously a mistake had been made, but how should I translate the ambiguity? If I corrected it, then Elza would be saying Alexis wanted her to run away with him 'at the time of the planting'—thus immediately after her father's death. And if I left it, then she would be saying that Alexis wanted her to run away with him 'at the time of the harvest'—thus, again, after, and well after her father's death.

'The problem is,' I explained to Louise, 'that although it's a detail, it is very important. Whichever way I translate it I virtually establish that Alexis didn't murder Elza's father since his only motive for killing the old man would be that Elza didn't want to leave her father. Alexis had to leave—the police were suspicious of him and he was due to be conscripted into the army. And he wanted Elza to go with him, but she wouldn't because she knew how much the villagers hated her father—her presence was his only protection against them. If Alexis wanted her to run away only *after* her father died, then he'd have no reason to kill him—'

'It sounds like the Film Board needs a lawyer not a translator,' Louise interrupted.

'Yes,' I said, not really taking this comment in. 'The point is that Alexis should have tried to persuade Elza to run away with him *before* her father died. Then, when he learns that she won't leave because of her father, he suddenly goes off and kills the old man ...'

'Mistakes in continuity and dialogue do happen,' said Louise, 'and get through into the finished film with nobody noticing them until some critic writes that the actor shot somebody right-handed in the first ten minutes and left-handed half an hour later.'

'The trouble is,' I said, 'I keep on feeling that if I knew who the murderer was then I would understand the film. And of course I can't translate the film properly until I do understand it.'

'But you said ...' (Louise by this time had heard a great deal about *Elza's Story*) '... that at the end, when the soldiers arrive in the village, it turns out to be irrelevant who has committed the murder because the Tsarist captain establishes that it's been a conspiracy all along. That's why there are so many possible suspects—to confuse the issue and stop one person being accused.'

'Even though it's a conspiracy, Louise, there's still a murderer. Somebody actually puts the knife into him and I want to know who that person is.'

She was looking at me.

'I know that I'm sounding obsessive,' I said. 'And I suppose I am. Stuart Cullen must know his business after all, because despite all the film's talk and obscurity I do find myself involved in it, in a strange sort of way.'

'I can see that,' Louise said.

After that she took to referring to *Elza's Story* as 'Erika's first case'. This used to embarrass me a little, but I was aware that I was spending an increasing amount of time thinking about the film. It always seemed to be the first thing in my mind when I woke in the morning.

It wasn't the small details that worried me, troublesome though they were; it was one particular scene, one that played over and over in my mind. This was the scene where the Tsarist captain and his men rode into the village to finally announce the result of their investigation.

In that scene the Captain takes over Elza's role as narrator. He dictates his thoughts in crisp sentences to a lieutenant who takes notes for the official report. The Captain speaks of himself in the third person. Following his cross-examination of the villagers he concludes that the murder is the outcome of a nationalist revolutionary conspiracy in which this entire village is implicated. The victim was employed by the Crown and the crime was politically motivated. Therefore (the Captain continues) this crime is an assassination ... and therefore it is treason. Ten ringleaders have been arrested; they have now been convicted of the crime by the military investigators ... The calm summary goes on and on. The gallows are set up and the ropes have been tried. The Captain is obliged to observe that due to the extreme cold, the ropes will snap and so the convicted will have to be shot. The scene then quickly fades to another where the executions are shown in the background; at that stage there occurs a conversation between the Captain and the lieutenant which shows that the Captain has lied in his report about the last detail: it isn't the weather that prevents the hanging, but rather the poor quality of the ropes purchased by the army.

This scene was one of the strongest of the film, but it was also perplexing. If I had been Balodis, I would have been more careful. As I was translating the Captain's cool conclusions, I wondered why none of the villagers, in their endless discussions of the murder and the murderer's motives, had ever referred to the possibility of a conspiracy. And, if there was a conspiracy, how, in that amazingly talkative village, had the conspirators managed to keep their mouths shut? Perhaps they'd known the truth all along and, as the Captain reported, all their speculations were a feint; but the villagers' concern about the crime had seemed too strongly characterised for me to believe that it could be entirely fabricated. Moreover, whenever the Captain gave them the opportunity to talk, their confidences just tumbled out and he could scarcely get them to shut up. But he didn't know how lucky he was. During his cross-examinations, the villagers were—for once—entirely consistent and accurate. They didn't muddle any dates or events, or misremember the names of any close relatives.

I often thought, as I was translating this section, that it was a pity it was at the end of the film. When the public finally got to see the translated version, they would have to spend hours battling with all the other minor confusions before they reached this. I wasn't looking forward to telling Stuart Cullen that his great soon-to-be-proclaimed masterpiece was riddled with such discrepancies.

Or so I thought until the morning when I saw the film for the third time. My intention had been to see it one last time to note the points I needed to resolve, but then I realised that something else was wrong. This concerned a scene which occurred in the middle of the film—the scene where Elza relates what she calls 'the latest developments' regarding her father's death to her cousin, Janis. I had listened to the conversation several times before and I hadn't been struck by anything odd. Elza simply tells Janis that her father has been found murdered in the schoolroom, and Janis announces to her that he has to go into the army. Janis adds that he would rather commit suicide than enlist.

Elza responds to Janis's despair in her usual fashion. She becomes excited by the drama of the situation and goes on to bigger things. Ignoring Janis's personal plight, she delivers an address on the morality of suicide.

I was thinking how much the intellectual Elza was enjoying the opportunity to get her teeth into this when I suddenly realised that her whole conversation with Janis could not have taken place. By the time that 'the latest developments' had occurred *Janis had already joined the army*. An earlier scene had shown his parents forcing him to enlist, just before Elza's father's murder. The film also showed Janis dying at Tannenberg, fighting the Germans, in 1915. Thus when he appeared in old age in the film—he was one of Elza's reconstructed survivors.

My first impulse was to leap up and ask Kevin if he could run the scene again for me, but I changed my mind. I knew that I hadn't made a mistake. It didn't even surprise me that I'd never noticed this anachronism before. The film was so full of rapid time-shifts which were intercut so quickly that you would have to know the scenario very well to notice the discontinuity. A first-time viewer could easily miss it.

'But surely not the director?' I said to myself as I walked back to my office. 'Surely not the person who made the film?'

Balodis himself had written the script. He *must* have known that this scene of Elza's conversation with Janis could not have occurred. And if Balodis hadn't noticed this glaring mistake, surely somebody else would have? The producer Leblenis perhaps, or one of the editors; it seemed impossible it could have slipped by all of them.

'But it did,' I said to myself, 'it did slip through. And it took *you* three viewings to notice it.' I told myself that Stuart Cullen would probably consider it unimportant; he would be full of tales of directors who'd left even more startling discontinuities in their films. In any case, even if he did think it was a serious matter, he would hardly consider it my fault. They don't shoot the translator, do they?

For the first time in all my weeks at the Film Board I was less than conscientious. Suddenly I wanted to get away. I decided that I was going to desert Peteris Balodis, Elza and the villagers. I was going to leave the Tsarist captain and his men to their own devices. I wasn't getting paid for this sort of agitation. It was all becoming too oppressive.

I rang in next morning and said that I was sick, then lay in bed reading a novel. However, I simply could not let *Elza's Story* alone. All the rest of that day my mind kept returning to that scene of Elza's conversation with Janis, trying to see if there was something I had missed, a connection I'd overlooked, but it was all in vain.

I had to talk to someone about the film. It could not be Stuart Cullen. Apart from the fact that I'd be unable to explain exactly what the problem was, I felt that he wouldn't pay any attention. I needed somebody more detached. I wished that Vince was not overseas.

Then I remembered Bill King, the editor. *He* was supposed to be working on the project. Any problems that I was having could end up making his job more difficult. Surely he ought to know what was going on?

This seemed a very satisfactory solution. I returned to my novel confident and happy.

CHAPTER 5

Amazingly, it only took one day to put my plan into effect. When I spoke to Bill King, he said immediately that he was very busy. I could feel his impatience as I tried—not very coherently—to explain to him the problems that *Elza's Story* was causing me. Then he interrupted and said that I ought to set up a screening of the film for him that very afternoon. I could provide a running translation and commentary as he watched.

My heart sank. It was obvious to me that Bill knew nothing about our complicated relationship with the Soviet consul.

Predictably the reaction at the consulate to my request to see *Elza's Story* within a day of an earlier screening was astonishment verging on shock. The consternation at the other end of the line was so great that I had to immediately invent a reason for the proximity of the screenings.

I said that the new screening was for the editor's benefit.

'The editor?' repeated the voice at the consulate. The voice was now becoming undecided.

'Yes, the editor,' I replied in a firm tone, 'the editor will need to see the film twice, in fact. Three days apart,' I added authoritatively. 'So *another* screening will be required for the editor in three days' time.'

'I shall have to refer this request to the consul,' said the voice again.

I refrained from saying, 'Inevitably.' Instead I said, 'Then please explain to the consul that the editor will need to see the entire film today and then again in three days.'

'Three days?' repeated the voice.

I knew that I was winning.

'For technical reasons,' I said.

I put the phone down feeling triumphant. The second screening had merely been a ploy to impress the consulate staff with the urgency of the situation, but now it struck me as an inspiration. Stuart Cullen would almost certainly wish to see the film again once he'd heard of my problems with it. I congratulated myself that I had killed two birds with one stone.

Even for his own special viewing Bill King didn't alter any of his habits. He was nearly an hour late; I paced up and down anxiously until it occurred to me to go off in search of him. I eventually discovered him chatting and drinking coffee in someone's office, and afterwards our progress to the theatrette was interrupted by so many neighbourly greetings that I began to despair we'd ever get to see the film.

I had already prepared, or to be precise, I'd attempted to prepare, a synopsis of *Elza's Story*, and I'd also made extensive notes on the various discrepancies and, in an additional couple of paragraphs, I had tried to convey why I was so concerned. I had expected that we would discuss these prior to seeing the film, but when we arrived Bill called out a cheery, 'Get her going, Kev!' and showed such indications of wanting to linger by the projection box that I dropped any thought of preambles and was relieved to get him into the theatrette, away from all distractions.

While the film was running I attempted to give a quick summary of its events and to point out some of the inconsistencies. At the beginning Bill sat with his head inclined towards me, his eyes on the screen, giving little nods as I talked. But as my explanations necessarily became more elaborate, I could feel his attention slipping.

At one extremely important point, he raised his hand to stop me so that he could concentrate on the screen. Then he said, 'Brilliant. You see that? Really brilliant. Stuns me.' I didn't know what he was talking about, but I nodded enthusiastically. 'Don't see much of it do you?' he remarked. 'Not as good as that anyway.' I nodded again and tried to remember where I was up to.

I embarked once more upon my explanations. For a while Bill seemed to listen. Then I noticed that he was nodding automatically. He was sitting further forward in his seat and becoming more and more excited as he watched. He was a very lively viewer. As the film proceeded, he started to twist around in his seat, to lean forward and peer intently, to jerk back again and then start the whole routine once more. At times there was more movement in the seat beside me than there was up on the screen.

Halfway through, I knew I'd made a mistake. It was pointless trying to continue my commentary. The film was too complicated, and my attempts to point out its discrepancies compounded the confusion. I could sense that Bill was getting irritated. His nods were becoming more abrupt. I started to feel flustered. My face began to flush with embarrassment.

I knew that Bill wanted me to stop talking. He was half-turned away from me now, so that I was addressing my unavailing remarks towards his averted head. Finally, I fell silent. I don't think Bill even noticed.

When the lights came on, he exclaimed, 'Brilliant, brilliant! Stuns me.'

We were rising from our seats. I forced my notes into his hands. But before I could say anything he went on, 'We'll have to have a talk about it, OK? I'll get in touch.'

I felt too defeated to contest this. I stood aside and let him go out ahead of me. As I was leaving I heard him chattering away with Kevin in the projection box.

Towards lunchtime the next day, as I was tidying up the draft of my translation, and writing accompanying notes, my phone rang. It was Ava.

'The Great Man requires your presence,' she said.

I was surprised to hear from her. I had been past her desk earlier and noticed her absence. I commented on this adding, 'I thought you were away sick.'

'*I'm* not,' she answered, 'but our receptionist is—and so I'm doing my job as well as hers for the day.' She sounded harassed.

'That's a bore,' I said sympathetically. I felt rather like a chat. I was tired of being alone in my office with Elza and Janis and Alexis.

'Yes,' Ava agreed, 'and of course this is the day on which everything else has to go wrong too. Vince was supposed to return last night so he could attend an important meeting today, but his flight was delayed so he's only just got in. We've been waiting all morning for an important phone call from Bob Basnett in Delhi but the connection is terrible and the call keeps dropping out each time he rings and there's so much going on that I can't even spare a minute to get away to get a cup of coffee.'

'Would you like *me* to fetch you a coffee?' I asked, adding, 'it won't take more than a few seconds.'

Ava laughed. 'Thanks,' she said, 'but you'd better see Stuart first ... seems to be in a terrible temper this morning.'

I was glad of Ava's warning because when I saw Stuart his manner was definitely odd. It wasn't until I had left him, though, that I was able to identify the way in which it was odd—then I realised he had stayed in his seat, he didn't walk around at all; and, more importantly, he was almost monosyllabic.

'I saw Bill King this morning.' There was displeasure in his voice. 'He says that you are having some difficulties with the translating.'

I too was annoyed. I didn't think that my problems with *Elza's Story* could be summarised simply as translating difficulties. But it was more than that: why had Bill King not discussed the matter with me, why had he gone straight to Stuart? I felt betrayed.

'Well,' I began, trying to imagine what Bill had said and where I ought to begin my explanation. I wasn't allowed to continue.

'Have you completed the translation of the entire film?' 'Yes,' I said, 'Of course ...' I stopped for two reasons. Firstly, amongst the papers on Stuart's desk I noticed the precis I'd given Bill

King, and secondly, it seemed obvious to me that anyone having problems with a translation would complete the text in the hope that later developments might help clarify the inconsistencies.

But Stuart was leaning forward to collect a folder from a tray. 'Could I see a full transcript by midway through next week?' he asked, adding that Ava would type it for me.

All his attention appeared fixed on the folder he had just picked up. His request was clearly a dismissal. Again saying of course, I left, wondering if Ava could enlighten me as to how, precisely, I'd given offence.

Ava, however, seemed to be having an even more difficult time than I was. At the reception desk the phone was constantly ringing. In the deepening lines of her face, strain was clearly showing: her pulled-back hair had slipped its moorings and tendrils were coming down around her eyes.

I quickly took in the scene and said, 'Put all the lines on engaged. They can do without the outside world for a couple of minutes can't they?'

She shook her head. 'I've booked a call through to Bob Basnett in Delhi and it should be coming through any second now.'

I was looking at the phone system.

'I know how to operate one of those,' I said. 'Why don't you go and have a coffee now? I can keep an eye on it for a couple of minutes.'

As she left me I eased myself into her chair and sat eyeing the lights on the switch panel. A light flicked off to indicate a disengaged line and then promptly flicked on for engaged again. I picked up the handset and sat all prepared: Come in Delhi. Then there was a light and a buzz and I informed an indistinct noise that I was the State Film Board of New South Wales. Then I heard Bob Basnett's voice asking faintly for Stuart. I hastily told him to hold and I was about to connect him to Stuart when I realised that the latter's line was engaged. I clicked his line open to interrupt him. I had the receiver against my ear.

I suddenly heard Stuart say: 'Very fluent in English.'

I closed the line, reconnected myself back to Delhi, told Bob Basnett to wait, and then I held my breath as I opened Stuart's line again:

'... more than a mess. He wonders if she knows what she's doing. She seems to be worried about all sorts of details and says that the narrative is full of mistakes, that it doesn't make sense. What I'm wondering is how fluent is she in the spoken language? She could have ...'

I never heard the end of the sentence. Ava was coming down the hall. My finger slid down and closed the line.

'Bob's waiting,' I said to Ava. 'He came through, then I lost him—perhaps you'd—'

Without any further explanation I vacated the chair. I saw Ava's surprised look, but she took the handset and it was her voice that Stuart heard, interrupting his conversation and connecting him to Bob Basnett.

Too numbed at first to fully credit what had happened, I headed back to my office, then stopped on the way at the women's toilet as the nearest refuge and sat in a cubicle. It was so unexpected. They didn't believe me. They thought that I could not do the job. It didn't make sense: if they thought that I didn't know what I was doing, how did they explain those detailed notes I had made? And as for Stuart Cullen's comment about me being worried about 'details', was I not supposed to be concerned about details? I'd been told, by *him*, to strive for perfection. It seemed as though I was simultaneously being accused of being incompetent and being overly zealous. Surely if I had been unable to do the job I would not have brought these 'details' to their attention? I would have bodgied up a translation and gone my own sweet way, confident they wouldn't know what a mess I'd made of things until another Latvian speaker saw *Elza's Story*. It was so unfair. I'd worked very hard. They'd condemned me without even attempting to hear me. Hurt and resentment brought tears to my eyes. I would have started to cry then and there in the toilet cubicle—but luckily I managed to remember that it was now practically lunch time: people would be moving about in the corridors very soon. I had to return to my office immediately.

Back at my desk I gathered together the pages of my translation thinking as I did so that there was really very little work remaining. I scarcely required until the middle of the following week to complete it. So much time was almost an insult, it was a reflection of Stuart Cullen's opinion of my competence. I then began to wonder what he intended to do with my completed draft. Was he planning to employ another translator to check my work? I had been standing while I sorted the papers on my desk. I now sat down. If the new translator confirmed that I was right, what was Stuart going to do then? Sack that translator and hire another? Disbelieve this next translator and do the same again ... until he'd run out of translators and finally begun to realise that there might be something seriously amiss with his great Latvian masterpiece?

All Stuart's battles had been predicated on the greatness of *Elza's Story*. I had come up with news he simply was not able to hear—and so he could only conclude the fault was with me rather than the film. It all became painfully obvious to me that afternoon, but still my mind teemed with questions. Why hadn't he and Bill King discussed the film with me? Why hadn't he proposed hiring another Latvian translator to aid me? Why was I being treated like this? Most of all it was their behaviour towards me that I couldn't bear. But I also could not separate the underhand means through which I had learnt their true opinion of me from the way I was being treated and I began to feel ashamed. I started to feel as if what had gone wrong had been, once again, my fault. The guilt I had felt earlier returned with renewed force. I should never have stayed here. I should have taken the Baltic group's protests as a warning. I'd been found out. They knew I was an imposter.

I was finding it impossible to concentrate. Great surges of hurt, guilt and humiliation would rise up in me every few minutes until I couldn't bear looking at the pages before me on which I had worked so hard. Other terrible thoughts kept coming into my mind. Other people would hear about this, Bill King was a great talker. Perhaps the story of my alleged incompetence was already known all over the Board. Perhaps a conversation was already taking place somewhere in which someone was saying that I'd lost my job, fired for incompetence.

I had to get away before I burst into tears. I hastily gathered my things and, having checked that the corridor was empty, hurried to the fire escape stairs because I knew that I could not avoid meeting people if I took the lift.

The fire escape stairs led, through a side door, into the main foyer of the building. I opened this door very quietly, having developed a sudden anxiety that I would walk straight into the foyer and meet Stuart Cullen or Bill King. But what happened was that I opened the door so soundlessly that the large man standing there, in my path, didn't realise I was there.

Until I said, 'Excuse me—oh, hello.'

Neath apologised and explained that he was waiting for Jacqueline while his slow grin spread over his big face. 'What're you doing?' he asked.

Cornered, I made a general gesture at the outer world.

'Going home.'

'It's too early.'

I was taken aback at this apparent show of bureaucratic punctiliousness on his part but I remembered his constant good nature and said lightly, 'It's four thirty-two. Traditionally this is the hour for translators of Latvian films to go home. Latvia is such a small country that if we worked right through to five o'clock, we'd soon run out of things to translate.'

Neath laughed. But it seemed to me he understood that

behind my ironic tone something was disturbing me because when he spoke, his tone was gentle.

'No, you've got me wrong, it's not too early to leave work, but it's too early to go home. Come and have a drink. It's Friday, Jacquie and Vince and I are going to the bar on the corner.'

My heart leapt with relief. I replied yes I'd love to come. I had forgotten about Vince Marcus being back in Sydney. He was the person I needed. He'd help me. I could imagine him listening to my account of Stuart Cullen's behaviour and muttering a weary curse. He would restore some sanity into this mad situation. He would go to Stuart and say, 'Are you going to hire a whole fleet of Latvians and then tell them that none of them can speak their native language?'

Neath, however, was chatting. 'How's your wonderful friend Louise?' he asked.

'Still wonderful,' I said.

'Somebody was telling me that the shooting of Paolo's film has been delayed again?'

The start of Paolo Sales's film in which Louise was to be the lead had become a sort of floating fixture. It now had a title, *Vampire's Gold*, but that was the only definite thing about it. Dates were always being made and unmade because of troubles with script and money. The latest delay had been occasioned by Paolo Sales's decision to hire a French actor to play the vampire.

'Entirely unknown outside his own village,' was how Louise had summarised Etienne Duprès to me. 'But once you set eyes on him, you'll see why his village is so keen to keep him a secret. He's delicious.'

I explained all this to Neath, adding that filming of *Vampire's Gold* was now supposed to start in about three weeks' time. Then I asked, 'How's *At Half the Asking* coming along?'

'Funny you should ask,' said Neath. 'Jacquie's upstairs in a meeting right now. No doubt having another showdown. She says it's like having a pregnancy that goes on for years. People keep asking.'

Right on cue the lift doors opened and Jacqueline herself joined us. Neath gave her a quick kiss as she announced:

'Vince says he'll be down in a couple of minutes.'

'Good, Erika's joining us.'

Jacqueline took in this news with a nod.

'How'd it go?'

Jacqueline shrugged. She'd had her hair cut very short in a severe style which I decided didn't suit her. It made her fine chiselled features look spare and stern. Now she stared away at the glass doors at the front of the foyer, plainly not wishing to talk. She raised her hand wearily to her forehead and pushed her hair back. It sat up in spikes as if it had been roughly cropped. The effect was very dramatic, I could easily see it: newly liberated France ... declared a Nazi collaborator ... large eyes, set pale face, hair shorn, public humiliation ... but wrongly accused ... carrying out espionage under the guise of consorting with German officers ... handing over floor-plans of the secret rocket installation to the doorman with her coat as she went into the nightclub ... martyrdom now.

Suddenly I wanted to leave. I felt that what I should do was enter the lift and reach out a hand and press the button and disappear behind the closing doors, like a character closing a scene in a play.

But Neath was saying, 'You know Vince's LA deal is definitely off?'

Jacqueline nodded. 'It's going to be a grim little cocktail hour tonight. Have you got some bad news to add to the occasion, Erika?'

I thought of saying, 'Plenty.'

When Vince joined us, it seemed generally understood that there were to be no references to the current state of anyone's career. This suited me, but several drinks on an empty stomach also helped. The upsets of my day shrank in importance when compared to the setbacks that Vince and Jacqueline had encountered. I gazed at them both sympathetically, hardly surprised that she should become impatient at a kindly meant enquiry about her film, or that he at times appeared so weary and disengaged. The strains they bore, I thought to myself, full of alcohol and hero worship and over-identification, the struggles they faced. In this mood it seemed to me that I could not even think of raising with Vince my minor plights concerning *The Story of the Year of 1912 in the Village of Elza Darzins*. He was sitting next to me. He looked pale and I remembered Ava saying there'd been delays with his flight. Looking pale became him. He had dark eyes and dark hair and squarish firm features. The pallor gave drama to his face.

Neath did most of the talking. I sat listening and occasionally taking part in the conversations in a marginal way until Vince leant forward and filled my glass and commented, 'I'm glad you're still here. I saw you staring into space a while ago and thought you might be bored and thinking of leaving.'

This was the moment when I could have altered the future. If I had replied no, I had not been bored, I'd been distracted because a scene from *Elza's Story* had suddenly come sharply into my mind, then everything that happened afterwards would have been different.

But I didn't explain this to Vince. When he'd leant forward to fill my glass his leg had brushed mine. So I paused briefly to consider his remark and to decide upon my response. Our legs remained touching.

'What happened in LA?' I asked. I'd been going to ask, what happened in Hollywood? But this didn't sound like an authentic question. It was more like a line from some chorus in a forgotten musical. What happened in Hollywood? What happened in Hollywood! What didn't happen in that wonderful town!

He smiled and said, 'What happened in Hollywood? Well, movies, movies, movies. But not for Yours Truly. And not for about half a million other aspiring directors I suppose. It didn't come off.'

'I am sorry.'

There was a long pause, but his leg stayed firmly against
mine.

I asked, 'Did they tell you why?'

He shrugged, smiled again and afterwards he reached over
and gave the back of my neck a little rub. Feeling self-conscious
I tried to think of something to say and my eyes alighted on
Jacqueline.

'Jacquie's also got big problems with her film?'

He nodded. 'Same problem,' he said. 'Nix bucks. The Film
Board have decided that they won't give her any backing.'

'So what happens now?'

He shook his head. 'Hard times. But she'll battle on. She's
been struggling with it for years now.'

I looked at Jacqueline again. She was smiling at something
Neath was saying, but when she ceased to smile she looked
drawn, exhausted. I felt Vince's hand giving me another friendly
pat on the back of my neck. I gave him a sideways look.

'Did you grovel to a mogul?'

'No, I just practised a lot in my hotel room.'

Jacqueline and Neath stood up to leave. Vince asked me quietly if I'd like a lift home. I quietly nodded that I would. I was in
a complete daze as I followed him out into the night.

In the car we sat for a moment in silence. Then Vince leant
over and laid his head upon my shoulder and closed his eyes.
His hair was warm against my neck. He opened his eyes:

'Come home with me?'

As soon as we entered his apartment Vince took me by the
shoulders, moved me back against the wall and standing there,
with his hands firmly on my shoulders, started to kiss me.
Eventually I raised my hands and wrapped his arms around
my waist. But he kept on kissing me for a long, long time and
later that night, as I lay beside him in bed, I reflected that this
single-minded concentration was one of his most appealing
characteristics.

CHAPTER 6

In fact it took me a long time that night to get around to Vince in my reflections. I spent the first hour after he had gone to sleep feeling unfettered. It was as though I'd been missing out on everything that was wonderful and now at last a new age was starting. I was full of retrospective sympathy for myself. If only I had known how well things were going to turn out when I'd been sitting in the women's toilets, on the verge of tears.

Finally, as I began to fall asleep I eased myself across the bed until I was nestled into Vince's warm body. I laid my cheek against his arm. All my immediate problems seemed settled— in my mind I had already prepared an amusing account of my difficulties with *Elza's Story* for his entertainment and I could easily imagine him laughing at my story while he worked out the best way of dealing with the matter. I had such a happy future laid out for the pair of us that I wished he'd wake up so we could start it immediately. But Vince had spent the previous night on the LA flight and he slept on determinedly. I would have to wait until morning.

I woke to see him squatting down beside the bed to dial the telephone. It was still early, the room was full of muted yellow light. I snuggled back under the bedclothes with the thought that I was going to have a hangover. It was a mild price to pay. In any case it was a Saturday, so I had the whole day to recover.

'Have you had enough sleep?' I asked as he began to dial again.

'Yes, thanks. I'm still on LA time. Damn, somebody must be telling their life-story.'

I counted the numbers, he was dialling international.

'You're going into the office today?'

He nodded. 'Got to catch up.'

Again he dialled and again he swore. I was glad he was having so much trouble. His morning-after attentions seemed, to
say the least, perfunctory. At the rate things were happening I
wasn't going to have much of an opportunity to tell him about
Elza's Story.

'Actually,' I began casually, 'I've got to do some work today
too. I'm having some trouble with—' But then I stopped,
abruptly: Vince was nodding and now he cut in.

'Yes,' he said, 'I know. Stuart was telling me yesterday.'

He was dialling again as he spoke, and his eyes were on the
telephone.

I felt myself go cold. I had not even thought about who had
been at the other end of Stuart Cullen's phone call. It hadn't
seemed important, but now it astonished me that I hadn't realised it was Vince. Bob Basnett was away in Delhi—so who
else was there with whom Stuart could discuss the case of the
unsatisfactory Latvian translator?

In a flash I now saw it all. There weren't going to be any accu-
sations. Nobody was going to call me in and say that my translation of *Elza's Story* didn't make sense. Stuart Cullen wasn't going
to admit, publicly, that he had made a mistake in hiring me. I
was going to be let go, quietly, and replaced.

And Vince, Vince ... who was to be my great protector ...
Vince hadn't even seen any need to raise the matter with me as
he took me to bed! For him I was just a night's entertainment.
There he was: a bit drunk, exhausted and bitterly disappointed
after his visit to LA, with the traditional diversion—a willing
woman. I was a transient, a peripheral person. I'd be gone by
the end of the week.

I stared at him, but he didn't notice. I rose to my feet, dressed
rapidly and without looking at him walked down the hall while
he was still beside the bed holding the telephone.

Now I was standing where I had stood the night before when
he'd taken me by the shoulders and started to kiss me. I didn't

move. I stood by the locked door and waited until he came down the hall to let me out. I didn't care what he was thinking or what he might say. I just wanted to go.

When he came down and unlocked the door I stepped past him and crossed the landing and went down the stairs without a backward glance.

The apartment that morning was very quiet. There was a note on the kitchen table from Louise saying she'd be away for a few days and leaving instructions about callers—but the phone never rang and nobody knocked. I am certain of that because I heard every creak and whisper in the old building.

For some hours I just sat on the sofa in the living room with a rug wrapped round me, too shocked to think. Towards the afternoon I cried myself to sleep. I woke up halfway through the night and stayed awake deciding what I would do.

My plan was to go to work and finish the draft of my translation for Stuart Cullen as quickly as possible. As soon as that was done, I thought it would only take a day or two, I would leave the office. I would ring Ava from the apartment to say the draft was on my desk ready for typing. And afterwards, quite simply, I wouldn't reappear. I would never go back.

They would be relieved to see the last of me. But I would have my revenge when they hired another Latvian translator and discovered I had been right all along. There *was* something very wrong with *Elza's Story*. I could see Stuart Cullen and Vince standing together with the next translator, shaking their heads and saying, 'That's what the previous translator said, but we thought that perhaps she couldn't understand it. You see, she hadn't had any professional experience: she only spoke Latvian because it was her mother's language.'

That Monday morning the Film Board offices seemed even more silent than the lonely apartment. I arrived very early so I could be in my office out of sight before Stuart Cullen and Vince appeared. But once I was at my desk the lack of the usual background hum of voices and telephones unnerved me. I couldn't concentrate on work. Even though I knew Vince was not going to come and enquire and that he and everyone else was going to pretend that nothing had gone wrong, I tensed each time I heard a sound.

Consequently I swung around as if I'd heard a rifle shot when suddenly there was an ostentatious cough in my doorway. It wasn't Vince. It was Kevin.

'It's here,' he said. 'For the first time ever in history, it's arrived when it was supposed to. With no hassles. I was so surprised when they brought it in I nearly fell off my chair.'

And with this he turned back and disappeared down the corridor towards the theatrette.

I, too, nearly fell off my chair. As I hastily rose to catch up with Kevin I stumbled and lurched forward. I could have laughed out loud at the sheer irony of it.

This was the first time the film had ever arrived without trouble. Every other screening of *Elza's Story* had involved a crisis of some sort, except this—the last, unnecessary, time. Then it occurred to me that this last pointless screening was the perfect refuge. Three hours alone in the screening-room with Elza Darzins. Perfect. I'd be safe. Nobody would walk in and find me crying. I could hide there in the darkness. As for my work, I would just have to take it home and finish it later that night.

In the theatrette there was enough light coming off the screen for me to move into a seat. The film was already starting. The room, unused for a few days, was chilly. I folded my arms and wished I'd brought a coat.

It was a moment before I was aware of the silence. Kevin had forgotten to switch on the film's soundtrack. I turned toward the beam of light coming from the projection box and called to him, but there was no reply. I rose and went out to see him, but the door to the projection box was ajar and the small room was empty. I assumed he would soon be back—so I sat down in a back row seat nearby, intending to go out shortly to see if he'd reappeared.

I still felt cold. I settled deep into the seat, my arms folded tight and my knees drawn up. The empty rows of seats stretched out before me, the red exit lights glowed over the doors at either side of the screen. I curled myself more tightly into the warmth of my seat, yawned and gazed at the red exit lights and then at the sprinkler vents in the ceiling. Then I began to count the rows of seats down to the screen.

Before me the film flickered silently. I knew its story so well that I could follow large parts of it at a glance and without the soundtrack. Elza was laughing. This was a happy period for the village. Elza was picnicking in the forest with her friend, Baiba, and Alexis. But shortly terrible things were going to happen.

I knew I should go off in search of Kevin but I didn't want to meet anyone so there was nothing to do except wait.

I contemplated my surroundings once more. For days now I seemed to have been in quiet places, but nowhere had been as quiet as this. Here it was utterly still. I closed my eyes. My head drooped and, at the movement, my eyes jerked open again.

That half-minute's slide into sleep woke me completely. I looked around to see if Kevin had returned but nothing had altered. On the screen the villagers still performed their silent actions—and I thought that here was another irony: my final viewing of this film was in silence, without dialogue, as if there had never been any words to translate. After all the trouble I'd had with its loquacious heroine and her talkative neighbours ... here they were, speechless at the end.

Elza's Story, I noted to myself after a while, actually made a fine silent film. As Peteris Balodis himself had said so often, the camera showed the movement. Now I understood what he was talking about. In my constant agitation over the film's mysteries, I had forgotten how good it was to watch: the isolated school-house across the empty field in the evening ... the old man moving about inside, lonely and vulnerable, unaware that his murderer was approaching ... he was stooped down now, replacing the children's slates in the cupboard by the blackboard ... The camera moved from left showing the teacher's high desk, then the blackboard on its pedestal and then, in the corner, the stiff old man returning the slates to the shelves. In the foreground was a bald stretch of pinewood floor, white from scrubbing.

I was too familiar with the murder scene that was coming to flinch from it, but my eyes moved away from the screen anyway. I saw the empty rows of seats beside me: there was no-one in those seats, no-one to stiffen as the old man turned away from the cupboard, no-one to witness the murder. But *he*—the old man—knew who his murderer was. Now he turned around, he was being stabbed in the chest. I saw him hunch and fall over, one hand clutching at the knife, the other reaching out towards the figure before him almost as though he was pleading for help. Then he was on the floor, both of his hands clawing at the knife now. His whole body began clasping up towards the wound. Then the knife was jerked out. He tried to raise himself, his hands covering the wound, and then, at last, he lay still.

I sat forward in my seat and began to say the dialogue softly to myself. The scene that followed took place in a cottage. Several men were seated at a table. At the end of the room were three women with their backs to the men, preparing a meal.

The men began to talk about the murder as a child came in crying. One of the women picked the child up, hushing him quickly—but in those few seconds while she was calming him her eyes were never once upon the little boy, her gaze was always fixed on the men. None of the women spoke a word yet it was clear they were all listening intently to what the men were saying. Their movements, as shown by the camera, were very circumscribed. They moved pots and utensils silently and fearfully. The whole village, I suddenly understood, was afraid.

'Yes,' I said to myself, 'the camera shows the movement.' Now Elza was opening a gate. As she slipped through it she looked around slowly and carefully while Alexis moved out from the shadow of the trees. Before them was a wide stretch of field and then the forest. Elza started to try to persuade Alexis to leave the village because he was in danger, but clearly she couldn't bear him going: as she talked, she did a sort of slow dance around him, stepping from one side to the other, taking his arm, releasing it, stepping back, standing still, facing him with hands held out. Then she reached forward and touched him on the chest, near the shoulder. At that he stepped back—but this was the only movement he made during the whole scene.

In the next scene Elza has just left the forest. The wide field lies before her once more and she walks across it in a straight line. I could recall this scene perfectly because it always irritated me. It shows Elza doing one of her performances as the village's resident philosopher. As she walks through the field she announces that the villagers do not understand what is happening. They see only facets; only *she* sees the whole. Whereupon she attempts to explain these broader perspectives to her mother. The camera shows the older woman to be terrified and grief-stricken: as Elza lectures her she gazes at this eaglet of ontology she's hatched as if wondering whether to be bemused or horrified ... But then the scene fades out to that of the arrival of the Tsarist officer and his men in the village.

They didn't look about them as they rode in. The camera showed them as totally indifferent, harbouring no curiosity whatsoever. Why would they waste their time looking at peasants? It was as if they already knew what sorts of secrets these peasants would be trying to keep.

Once the Captain and his men arrived, it didn't seem to matter who had been murdered, who had committed the murder, or why. The story was all there in the silent movements of the soldiers and the villagers. The villagers lined up silently for their identification. There was snow on the ground. The day was clear but the bitter weather was apparent in the way every person's hands and feet moved constantly to ward off the cold.

The Captain asked his questions, but his attention was more on his restless horse than on the villagers' replies. Ten young men were led away. The villagers stood about. The Captain's contempt for them was as powerful as the charge sheet he held in his gloved hand. Balodis's camera didn't sympathise with the villagers, nor did it condemn the Captain. Their helplessness, and his contempt, were simply part of the order of things.

And so was the justice the Captain was dispensing. This justice had nothing to do with the crime. The Captain had no interest in past events. The villagers' speculations, their suspicions, their fear and their guilt were of no importance to him. The more the villagers became immersed in telling him about the crime, the more the camera showed his lack of concern.

The law the Captain was supposed to be dispensing wasn't about justice, it was about authority; and this, I understood now, was why the survivors were still obsessed forty years later. They *still* wanted justice. For the murder was the one great event in the villagers' lives. It had destroyed their community. After it had taken place nothing would ever be the same again. Yet the murder was also, for the survivors, the last time they were to actively participate in any event that affected them. Everything that occurred afterwards would be determined by circumstances beyond their small world: death and destruction would arrive for reasons outside their control.

I saw it all finally. The Captain was the augur of the future. He had no concern with who had committed the murder; nor with the victim, nor with the crime itself. He was happier to shoot ten innocent men rather than one guilty one. And so the villagers themselves had tried to resolve the matter. With their constant gossiping and speculation they had acted as both investigators and jury. They had weighed up all the suspects and at the same time they'd tried to decide if the crime was justified. But they made the tragic mistake of assuming that the Tsarist State, in the person of the Captain, was concerned with justice too—whereas its only interest was in re-establishing control. So the State didn't want a murder committed by an individual. It wanted a well-organised conspiracy that could be seen to be uncovered and punished. All the information that the villagers so willingly gave thus helped the State to establish that the whole community was implicated. The ten young men were shot. As Balodis had said, his film was about 'the peculiar tragedy of the peasants'.

I was sitting forward staring so intently at the screen that it was some minutes before I realised that the film had ended. I had been completely absorbed by it. The ending was so precise. Everything came together to produce the final disaster. Now I was full of pity for the villagers. I knew now what happened in *Elza's Story*.

As I was leaving, Kevin appeared at the door of the projection box. 'You didn't have no vocals,' he said.

I nodded and smiled vaguely and hurried away. Back in my office I sensed that if I stayed in the building I would lose this new, fragile understanding. One thing, though, became clear to me as I gathered my papers: I was feeling inspired. In fact I was determined to do as perfect a translation as possible of *The Story of the Year of 1912 in the Village of Elza Darzins*.

CHAPTER 8

When I returned to the flat I decided that before beginning work I would write a series of notes on those parts of the film that most perplexed me. I was determined to translate these sections as well as I could. They might have to remain unaccountable, but at least they would be well-expressed and unaccountable. Even if I had to work all night and all tomorrow and all the next night, I was going to do my best by Peteris Balodis.

I knew now what had gone wrong with his film. He had had a great vision—'the peculiar tragedy of the peasants'—that in parts he'd been unable to sustain, but I felt his had been an honourable failure. 'Balodis,' I told him as I sat down at my desk, 'you've got my full support.'

I began writing my detailed comments very neatly, but I soon realised it was not what I wanted to do. I wanted to write my own version of *Elza's Story*. As I was watching the film, I knew I could tell the story as it *should* have been told.

I had no idea of how to go about this. A whole movie seemed an unimaginably vast project, and my only imaginative writing so far consisted of a number of narratives that came to a halt after three and a half pages and several hundred attempts at the definitive first sentence. But I crumpled my notes and threw them in the wastepaper basket and began an outline which I completed in just a few hours. Some parts I worked out in detail but mostly I wrote in quick rough sentences—leaving blanks in places where it was obvious to me what had to be done, and putting query marks in places which worried me but which I was sure I could resolve later on. I felt very confident. All my thoughts seemed to form so clearly and so rapidly ... and I soon understood why: they were all, in fact, very familiar to me. All my talks with Louise about the film, all my private parodies of Elza's monologues, all my questioning of the film's development ... I now knew what I'd been doing.

Unconsciously, I'd been rewriting *Elza's Story* for weeks.

Now all that was required was that the framework would hold—and it was holding. As I went on, I could see earlier sections which had worried me now falling quietly into place. I now felt fully convinced that what I was doing was right. *This* was the story. *Elza's Story*.

I was also astonished, and very proud, of my achievement. In the past my feeble, occasional attempts to carry on my fictions beyond the point of initial inspiration had always failed. Each time I would always be hopeful of producing something grand and significant, but each time—very quickly—I'd end up with something strained and faltering. When I looked at what I'd written, I would perceive it as part of some whole, but I could never envisage what that whole was. I would constantly remind myself that all writers faced this problem and that they all said you must persevere, you couldn't merely wait for inspiration, you had to go to your desk at regular hours and struggle to write regardless. I knew the hours of work of every great writer who'd had the foresight to have them recorded, but arriving at my desk at the same times as Flaubert, Tennyson or Baudelaire didn't seem to make any difference. Even my carefully reworked pieces seemed lifeless in comparison to the stories that constantly went on in my mind.

But I *had* been making up stories all my life ... It never occurred to me that this had any relation to the grand and proper business that I imagined writing to be—until that night when I rewrote *Elza's Story*. Then I realised that writing was what I'd been doing for as long as I could remember. The discovery delighted me. *This*, then, was how it was done. This was the world transformed.

So I felt doubly grateful to Peteris Balodis and even more determined to produce a fine translation of his film. I had already noticed from my earlier draft that there were a number of places where my confusion about what I was translating had affected my expression—and I began to do some careful editing. I told myself that even if I couldn't resolve the many oddities of the plot, at least I could underplay them and rely upon the visual power of the film to do the rest. I worked away steadily, shaking my head now and again over my more awkward renderings.

One long monologue of Elza's was especially tedious and confusing in the original—and, in my translation, not much better. It occurred to me that with a few rearrangements this monologue could become quite passable. All I had to do was move the last two sentences to the beginning and conclude the passage with the philosophical remarks which originally were in the middle. The thought did come to me that possibly I shouldn't tamper with the actual text, even to alter it so humbly, but I proceeded nonetheless, justifying my action with the argument that I wasn't denying the audience a single one of Elza's numerous reflections, I was only re-ordering their sequence. Afterwards the speech seemed much improved.

But much of the soundtrack consisted of Elza's speeches, either as monologues, voice-overs or in conversation—so it was easy to go from amending one to amending more. In the course of doing this, I found to my surprise that I was starting to like Balodis's narrator-heroine. Elza certainly *looked* the part (she was played by a young and very expressive actress) but instead of being brave and wise and tragic—as I thought the heroine of a great film ought to be—she was vain and silly and she was constantly showing off. And then, in the middle of rephrasing one of her monologues so that it would sound less like a passage from a badly written Marxist primer, I suddenly understood the importance of this constant showing-off on Elza's part. In a real sense *The Story of the Year of 1912 in the Village of Elza Darzins*—the film itself—was her attempt to come to terms with the most important event of her past. No wonder the film contained so many monologues and voice-overs, and no wonder it appeared inconsistent. Elza Darzins, I discovered, was one of those famous fictional characters who write themselves. The film was *her* story.

Once begun, my revisions were such that it was only a small step from amending Elza's speeches to bringing in structural changes which would improve the coherence and cohesion of the whole film. The rewrite now amounted to quite a number of pages, but I happily continued working. I looked at it fondly and said: 'Let's see how long we can keep this show on the road.' I made a few deletions, then I turned a few ambiguous statements into more definite ones ...

And the villagers became more consistent. Confident that it all made much better sense in my version, I rewrote substantial parts of the dialogue to clearly show how dangerous the large number of suspects made the situation—something which then could account for the villagers' excessive volubility. If there had only been one or two possibilities, the little community could have found who the murderer was—thereby easily resolving the matter. But with *five* suspects (excluding Alexis, whose innocence I established definitively), each of whom was desperate to protect himself, and with everyone in the village aware that one ill-chosen word could incriminate an innocent man, the murder of the old man could only assume the dimensions of a major crisis. This was why the villagers started to disbelieve one another and to plot against one another, and this was why they were so willing to tell everything they knew to the Captain.

Another important change I made was the ending. In the film the murder is deemed by the Captain to be a conspiracy. Yet every circumstance about the murder indicated that it was the act of an individual. In my rewrite the Captain, for reasons of political expediency, took advantage of the villagers' cooperation to make it *appear* as though there had been a conspiracy. The climax of the film now was the Captain's sheer lack of interest in who had actually committed the crime. You could see his indifference to the matter in his movements on the screen.

'Balodis should have employed me as his scriptwriter,' I told myself. As Vince had said, he certainly knew how to aim his camera and I was now confident that I knew what his film was about. We made a great team, the pair of us, together—or, rather, we made a great team apart.

As I was writing I kept getting struck by the contrast between the clarity of Balodis's vision on the screen and his apparent inability to express himself in words. I was aware of course that this is not unusual, but every evening after composing and executing those wonderful scenes, Balodis had dictated his thoughts and reflections to his 'shooting diary'—those endless hours of cassettes in which he'd never made a single informative or substantial remark. Now I had another sudden illumination: there was indeed nothing of substance in the 'shooting diary'; and that, precisely, was the point! It explained why there had been so little interference from the Soviet authorities during the making of Balodis's films. What could be more useful to the Soviet agent, planted in the production crew to ensure the orthodoxy of the film, than a daily record of the director's private thoughts and reflections?

Looking back I am astonished that I did not construe that demanding and careful fabrication of Balodis's as a warning of the dangers surrounding the project in which I had now involved myself. At the time I was too elated and triumphant for such a thought to occur to me. As I gathered the pages of my rewrite I only saw Balodis's duplicity as further proof of my conviction that all this was meant to be.

A chain of events had come together: the refugee woman's daughter, the story from the lost country, the artist unable to achieve his goal and the daughter, taught Latvian by her mother, able finally to do justice to the story of the lost country.

Elza's Story had become my story.

PART TWO

SCRIPTDOCTOR

LATVIAN LESSON

SIR: I must comment on J. Baird's assertion that Kings always beat Queens in card games. Apparently the writer has not heard of the most popular card game amongst Latvians—'Zolite'. In that game the Queens always win. The Queen is the top card, followed by Jacks. Kings have no chance—even a lousy 10 of diamonds beats them hands down.

J Saks

(from the correspondence columns of the *Sydney Morning Herald*)

CHAPTER 9

When I first decided that I would write an account of *Elza's Story* I assumed that writing the narrative would be a simple task: after all, every event of significance had been recorded in my diary, so it seemed to me that all I had to do was to reconstruct my story. In the first half of the narrative, this turned out to be indeed the case. Events would occur, and I would react.

But the second half of my story soon became more complicated—and my diary reflected this. To begin with, my entries became longer—and longer. Yet they were also less substantial in a strange way. It was as if I was no longer quite sure what significance a day's events would have for me. Slowly I became aware of the difficulty.

In my diary I was unable to come up with a precise resolution to my quandary, but I did at least envisage what sort of person I ought to be to deal with it. On a number of occasions through the following months I wrote that what I needed in my life was somebody like Elza Darzins. I could see her amassing all the facts about all the events that were to befall me and talking, talking, talking her way through the problem. She would have pointed out that during this period I was always hoping that someone would come along and rescue me. First I had—briefly—turned to Vince. Now I would allow myself to be taken over again by Louise, to be swept along into her adventures.

In an authoritative voice-over Elza would have been able to point out the big difference between Louise and me. We had, she would have said, dissimilar needs. What Louise wanted most of all was to become a star. She had the talent; and all she needed from the world was the opportunity to display it. What *I* wanted from the world was something far more complicated.

I needed legitimation of my rewrite of *Elza's Story*.

I wanted to believe that rewriting the film had been necessary, inevitable and right. So when, a few weeks later, I discovered that all films are written and rewritten and always subject to change and reinterpretation and that, moreover, I had a facility for rewriting them, I felt completely undermined. I was even more disturbed when I realised that my talent was undiscriminating. In the coming weeks I was to go from rewriting *Elza's Story* to rewriting a trashy spoof of a vampire movie.

I would imagine Elza Darzins handling this metamorphosis with her usual aplomb. At the end of a long monologue on my rapidly changing circumstances, she would have simply pointed out, with characteristic unselfconsciousness, how Karl Marx had written somewhere that in history all events have a habit of starting out as tragedy and turning into farce.

As it was, immediately after my rewrite of *Elza's Story* I remember analysing the situation in a cool logical manner. My version of *Elza's Story*, I anticipated, would have two tests to face. The first of these was Stuart Cullen. I wasn't sure how thoroughly he knew the film, but I suspected that his understanding of the plot—beyond the generalities—was extremely limited. I concluded that he would dismiss as unimportant any discrepancies between his memories of the screening in Moscow and the translation he was soon to read. I remembered that he had never said anything specific about the content of the film and that when he'd learnt of my difficulties with it he had not attempted to discuss the matter with me. 'As he would have done if he really knew the film,' I told myself. 'If you knew the film and you had declared yourself as obsessed about it as he has, then you would want to at least discuss it. You would want to know exactly what the problem was.'

As for the second test, if it was applied there simply wouldn't be any hope either for my rewrite or for me. If the State Film Board hired another Latvian translator to check my work, the first thing which that astonished person would tell them was that my subtitles of *Elza's Story* in no way resembled the soundtrack. And that, as they say, would be the end of the matter. There would be no way in which I'd be able to defend, or to redeem, myself.

I decided I should risk both tests, but up until the last moment I kept open the option of presenting my first translation. It had sat neat and tidy and almost complete on the desk beside me as I worked all night on its usurper, and I also had it in my folder the next morning when I stood at Ava's desk. I knew I was going to give her my new, my own version. I suppose I thought I could still change my mind—even as I was handing my version to her I could say, 'Oh, I've muddled the drafts, sorry, here's the latest one.'

My hand trembled but my voice was steady as I placed the new draft in Ava's in-tray. She seemed to be looking at me attentively and I felt sure she'd heard of Stuart Cullen's misgivings about me—but all she said was: 'I won't actually be able to start typing it until this afternoon. If you want to look over it again, do so. I'm always finding that people remember they meant to alter something after they've given the copy to me.'

I stopped myself from seizing it immediately. Instead I gave the in-tray a rueful glance and heard myself saying in one breath, 'Oh no, that's not necessary, I've already double-checked it you see.'

Now I realise I was doing precisely what Ingmar Bergman said you should do when making a film, 'Make every movie like it's going to be your last.'

I didn't know then that *Elza's Story* would hardly be my last movie. I spent the rest of that day, and the next, nervously pacing the apartment. Louise had returned, but the shooting of Paolo Sales's movie was finally about to begin; and she was very busy, flitting in and out at all hours.

My excitement had sustained me until I'd handed over my rewrite to Ava, but once that was done I was desperate to be away from the Film Board in case I lost my nerve. I also wanted to avoid running into Vince. So I told Ava I thought I was getting a cold and would take a couple of days off. As I walked restlessly from room to room I wondered if there was already another Latvian translator sitting at my desk listening to the soundtrack of *Elza's Story* and reading my subtitles and getting more and more bewildered. I decided that if a phone call came telling me I'd been found out I would simply admit everything—including eavesdropping on Stuart Cullen's phone call to Vince—and then they could do with me as they wished.

But I hoped that I wouldn't be found out before the Sydney Film Festival. I'd heard from Ava that Stuart was planning to hold a special by-invitation-only preview screening of *Elza's Story* for overseas guests and local critics and other persons of note prior to the Festival itself. Now my heart became set on this preview. It seemed unlikely that any speakers of Latvian would be attending it and what I wanted was just one screening under normal conditions, when an audience saw *my* version of the film. I knew of course that once the truth came out the print with my subtitles would be destroyed. But one audience, one audience only for my *Elza's Story*, I decided, and I'd be satisfied.

When I returned to the Board I tried to refrain from going immediately to Ava, but I was scarcely out of the lift before I was at her desk. She half-laughed, half-shook her head at me.

'Oh dear, you are a worrier aren't you? Stuart is absolutely delighted ... he can't stop talking about it.'

'He thinks it looks OK?' I broke in. 'He's satisfied?'

'Satisfied? He couldn't be more pleased if he'd done it himself,' she said smiling. 'But why should I tell you what he will tell you—at so much greater length—himself? He'll be in shortly.'

I attempted to take this news as casually as possible. I even asked a casual question, 'Have you seen Vince yet this morning?'

Ava looked at me in surprise. 'Didn't you hear?' she asked. 'He's gone back to LA.'

The American studio had changed its mind and called Vince back for further talks. The message had come the day after he'd returned to Sydney, and he had flown out early the next Monday morning. I remembered the phone calls at his flat and smiled to myself wryly: while I'd been sitting in my office that morning, tensing at every sound, he had been in a plane high in the sky, bright in the morning sunshine, flying to LA.

A couple of hours later Bill King appeared in my doorway. 'Trying to do me out of a job?' he enquired. He moved into the room, talking non-stop. 'As I was saying to Stuart last night, it's a pity you can't speak any other languages because you've got a great feel for dialogue. Lots of subtitles read like instructions to open soap packets, but it would be no trouble to get you a job doing it full-time. Sure, I know you were a bit of a Nervous Nellie there for a bit—couldn't work out for the life of me what was worrying you—but I always reckon it's better to have somebody who goes overboard on the worrying than ...'

Later I discovered that Bill had already been praising my version of *Elza's Story* around town, telling everyone that the film was going to be a hit, a very big hit. And people were very interested to hear this. Vince hadn't been alone in his criticisms of the amount of time and energy that Stuart Cullen had directed towards obtaining the Balodis films, so much so that there was now a joke amongst local film-makers that the only way you could win the support of the Director of the State Film Board of New South Wales was by relocating to some minor Soviet Socialist Republic and getting suppressed. All the glowing earlier reports of *Elza's Story* had originated with Stuart himself and there had been a not unnatural tendency to discount his views. Bill King's opinion, however, was neutral; his judgment was respected. When he started to praise *Elza's Story* everybody listened attentively. Then they began to talk.

Suddenly there was a change of attitude towards me in the corridors of the Film Board. People looked when I passed. They smiled and nodded. They said they'd heard the Balodis film was looking great. They said it was a pity about the other two films not being screened. They asked if Balodis was making another movie. There was a sort of permanent current of warmth around whenever I left my office. It terrified me.

I realised only too well that all this interest meant that things would be even worse when the truth came out—just as quickly the same people would then feel very differently towards me. I started to panic: on my way home I would drop into the local library to study law books. I consulted volume after volume, read countless cases ... but nonetheless I was unable to decide even upon what *category* of legal offence my crime could be assigned to. It seemed to hover on the borders of fraud, forgery and false representation. I spent hours deliberating whether what I'd produced was 'spurious'; certainly my version of *Elza's Story* was not 'counterfeit', but might it not be considered as 'passing off'? On the other hand it wasn't, strictly speaking, an act of 'deception for profit', or was it?

Eventually I gave up. What would be, I said to myself, would be. At least I was prepared for the worst.

Nothing, however, prepared me for what was to follow. One morning, tired and shaky after a sleepless night, I was greeted as soon as I arrived at the Film Board by an excited Stuart Cullen. He was waving a copy of that morning's newspaper.

'Have you seen this?' he demanded jubilantly. 'The front page!'

I hadn't seen the paper. The article was low down the page but sizeable. World premiere, it said. Suppressed masterpiece to be seen only in Sydney. Film festivals all over the world envious of Sydney's achievement. As I was reading Stuart remarked that organisations like the State Film Board usually only ever appeared on the front pages of the major newspapers if they were in danger of collapsing—or else the subject of a scandal.

'The two events often occur simultaneously,' he added.

I thought his last remark to be particularly ill-omened. I

could instantly imagine—all too easily—what a wonderful sequel the story of my rewrite of *Elza's Story* was going to provide. First the scoop, then the scandal.

'Very, very welcome publicity,' Stuart was saying.

He too, evidently, was not prepared for what was to follow. For later that day a new edition of the same newspaper reported that representatives of Sydney's Latvian community were denouncing the screening of *Elza's Story* as the centrepiece of the entire Festival. A press release from a group called the 'Baltic Peoples Union' had been issued. It noted that several weeks previously, the Minister for the Arts, Mr Sidney Everard Morris, had agreed that the screenings of Balodis's films were an outrage to the feelings of the local Latvian community and that he had directed the cutting back of the program. The press release concluded by stating that the Baltic community now realised that submissions to the Minister were pointless and that they were going to take 'direct steps' to ensure that *The Story of the Year of 1912 in the Village of Elza Darzins* would not be screened at all.

I read this news with relief, but also regret. The Baltic group's threat, I thought, would surely mean the cancellation of the screenings and the prompt return of *Elza's Story* to the USSR. I was disappointed that my version of the film would never now receive even its one screening, but also delighted to be saved in this way from the consequences of my act. Again, however, any feelings I might have had were quickly superseded by the next, rapid sequence of events. In the first place Minister 'Eisteddfod' Sid Morris declared himself thrilled by the public interest in *Elza's Story* and suddenly became a great champion of anti-censorship. He immediately issued a statement announcing that he had no intention of altering, in any way, the arrangements already made with regard to the screening of *The Story of the Year of 1912 in the Village of Elza Darzins* at the Sydney Film Festival.

The Baltic group was obviously waiting for this. That night a crowd of orderly people dressed in mourning gathered at the Pool of Remembrance by the War Memorial in Hyde Park, holding candles and singing hymns in front of television cameras while a pastor read out the thousands of names of those Latvians who were known to have been executed or deported or who otherwise had disappeared during the first Soviet occupation of Latvia in 1940. At the base of the stairs leading to the Memorial was a coffin with a Latvian flag draped over it. When the crowd departed they placed their candles in rows upon the grass. The last frames of the evening's television news showed these small memorials still flickering in the black sea of the park.

It was very effective. My throat constricted as I watched. I had agreed with Stuart Cullen that Balodis's film required a translator who wasn't too 'right-wing', but it was difficult for me to remain disengaged. Next morning there was an almost palpable air of crisis at the Film Board as Stuart struggled to find a way of soothing the Minister. Eisteddfod Sid, I learnt, was now wavering as the champion of free speech and was even thinking of cancelling the screening of *Elza's Story*. So, I thought, the film wouldn't be screened after all. I was in my office working with Bill King on the editing of the subtitles when Ava rang to ask me to go to the Director's office immediately.

As I walked in Stuart Cullen leapt up from behind his desk and placed an arm around my shoulders and ushered me into a chair. In sentences longer and more sweeping than any I had ever previously encountered, he then explained that he was obliged to terminate my employment. Immediately.

The phrases 'against my deepest wishes', 'a most immense and saddening development', 'an unfortunate situation beyond the power of any of us to, on either a collective or individual basis, rectify', rolled off his tongue while I digested what all this signified. I wasn't being dismissed from the Film Board because I'd been found out about *Elza's Story*. I was being dismissed because its Director had become fearful that the Minister would discover I was still working for the Board—in which case the

Minister would conclude that the Director had never been as whole-hearted about reducing the Board's commitment to the Balodis films as he'd appeared to be in the first place.

Bill King was indignant when I returned to my office and told him. He began pacing the room and shaking his head and saying he didn't know what the world was coming to.

'What are you going to do?' he asked. He sounded so genuinely concerned that I promptly felt, again, very guilty. His concern brought home to me how shocked he would be when he found out what I'd done.

'It's all right,' I said, trying to cheer him up. 'Louise's new movie starts next week, so at least there will be some cash in the household—'

I stopped because suddenly he stood up.

'Do you know where Louise is?' he asked.

'Right now?'

He nodded.

'I think she's at the photographer's—that's where she said she'd be going this morning. Then there's a lunch Paolo Sales is giving ...'

'I'll be back in a bit,' said Bill. 'Hang around.'

I hung around. I had some editing to finish on the subtitles and my desk had to be cleared out and tidied. A few minutes later the phone rang. It was Louise.

'You're unemployed, I hear, so you're coming to lunch,' she said peremptorily, giving the two statements equal weight.

'I can't ...' I began. Then Bill reappeared in the office. He summarily took the receiver from me. There was a moment's silence at our end of the line then he said, 'I'll bring her. Fifteen minutes, right?'

Lunch was at an Italian restaurant. As Bill and I went through the door I remembered that morning weeks ago in Vince's office and Neath saying, 'According to Paolo Sales you shouldn't have dinner in an Italian restaurant, you should only have lunch in an Italian restaurant.'

Louise hadn't arrived. Paolo Sales's eyes went over me automatically as Bill introduced us and we took our seats.

I stared back, curious. Paolo Sales was thin and dark with a narrow head and dark, fast-moving eyes which darted everywhere as he talked. But he appeared to be addressing me.

'I've spent most of the morning on the phone to Paris talking to Etienne Duprès's agent,' he began. 'Etienne gets here tomorrow for the vampire film, but I'm also thinking of contracting him for another project I'm developing. It's a thriller set on a beautiful palm-fringed Pacific island. It's very a promising project, but it still needs some work done on the script.'

I nodded. I couldn't understand why Paolo Sales was providing me with this information, but the morning's events had been so extraordinary that if he had remarked on what sunny weather we were having while outside the streets were full of driving rain I would have simply agreed. Paolo Sales continued:

'I'll get John Dowell to direct, he's directing *Vampire's Gold*. He's good on action. You can waste a lot of money there with people who don't know what they're doing. Mandy Soames is our Production Manager. She's good too.'

I was told all this unsmilingly so I nodded unsmilingly back. This seemed to encourage Paolo Sales because he then proceeded to explain to me that he never wrote his scripts yet all his films were always based upon his own original ideas. Thus the founding vision for the spoof vampire film had come to him during a night on the goldfields in the eerie Australian bush. As he walked through the bush, Paolo Sales had seen long black shadows, vertiginous mineshafts slashed deep into the ground ... and all around he had also seen drunken gold-diggers collapsed in stupor beneath the white and ghostly eucalypts with

their throats exposed in the moonlight to the stalking of an escaped convict with a Transylvanian background.

The film was to be shot at Hill End, a historic nineteenth-century village in western New South Wales—sunken mineshafts,
ghostly white gums, abandoned graveyards. I was to hear Paolo
Sales relate his bared-throats-in-the-moonlight vision often
thereafter but at the time I wasn't listening. I was more interested
in his manner than his words. He surprised me. He was certainly
no more pleasant than his hostile advance press (in the form of
Jacqueline Paley) suggested—clearly he *was* sharp, vulgar and
a confidence man—but his manner was unexpected and the
only word I could find to describe it was an old-fashioned, even
Victorian, expression. I decided that Paolo Sales was unbend-
ing. I was also beginning to realise he wasn't vouchsafing me all
these details about his productions and John Dowell and Mandy
Soames and so on merely as a substitute for small talk.

I listened without comment as he moved on to tell me more
about his other film, the thriller set on the palm-fringed island.
I kept feeling that an interview was taking place in which Paolo
Sales was reading both the questions and the answers from an
autocue over my shoulder. My silence must have struck Bill
King, who interrupted Paolo to say, hinting heavily:

'This thriller sounds a great idea, don't you think, Erika?'

But all I could do was nod silently once more. My only
thought at the time was to wonder why Paolo Sales kept insisting on calling his island 'palm-fringed'. I thought all Pacific
islands were palm-fringed.

Then Paolo Sales announced abruptly that he was looking
for an extra production assistant who could do general office
work, but who was also interested in reading and assessing film
scripts.

'Bill was telling me you write good tight dialogue,' he said.
'Also that you're a hard worker and you pick things up fast. I
need a good worker and your Latvian background will be useful too.'

I looked enquiring.

'For the vampire,' he explained.

I said that I thought vampires lived further south.

It emerged however that Paolo Sales didn't think that such details were important. (Later I learnt that this was typical of him.) Any part of Europe, outside the major centres, was much like any other, he explained, and in any case, he added, wasn't the film set in Australia?

I was too impressed by this sweep of logic to object. Across the table Bill King was watching me intently. It now became apparent to me, at last, that he was responsible for this offer of employment—indeed that he had arranged it all with Louise's help. When he met my gaze, he smiled happily.

Once again I felt the full irony of the situation. Bill King, who had inadvertently precipitated me into all my troubles with *Elza's Story*, who had helped bring about my impending downfall ... Bill King now had rescued me with a new job—at least temporarily. I reflected that Paolo Sales would undoubtedly sack me when the truth about *Elza's Story* emerged, but what did it matter? With luck, it would be three months before I was exposed, and I had to live in the meantime.

The world was both dangerous and funny. I told Paolo Sales I would accept his offer. He replied that I'd be working chiefly with Mandy Soames, and then stopped. 'Here she is,' he said.

Louise was making her entrance and, as usual, people were turning to look at her.

Later, during lunch, I whispered the news to Louise. She pretended to be surprised and passed word on to Bill, who also feigned amazement then beamed at me and said:

'Haven't had such good news since me rich auntie took sick.'

CHAPTER 10

This mood of amused detachment didn't last long. In fact I started work for Paolo Sales feeling like someone taking up residence in a city about to undergo enemy bombardment. I tensed every time the phone rang (and it rang all the time) expecting each call to be news of my exposure at the Film Board. I worked hard simply to take my mind away from my constant fear and apprehension. Whenever my attention wandered from the task at hand I would see Stuart Cullen's astonished face, the aghast Film Board staff, the articles in the media, the court case, my mother crying ...

Each night I studied the papers and the television news programs for reports on the Baltic group's campaign, but it appeared that a tacit truce was operating. The day I left the Film Board the Minister released a statement stating blandly that his Department's commitment to the Balodis films was being reviewed and that he was about to have discussions with representatives of the Latvian community. At the Film Board it was considered that he would make concessions in return for a halt to the public protests.

My chronic anxiety was a great asset in my new career. I did as I was told with the maximum amount of speed and the minimum amount of comment. My job consisted of helping Paolo Sales and Mandy Soames finalise arrangements for the production of *Vampire's Gold* which was now due to start shooting during the week. Later I discovered that Paolo Sales was short of money and was rapidly making adjustments to cut his costs— but at the time I simply made the hundreds of phone calls as directed by Mandy without reflecting upon anything other than the business at hand. I soon decided that my knowledge of Paolo Sales and his enterprises could best be described as a state of expanding ignorance. This didn't concern me: I was constantly expecting my employment to be temporary.

Worrying all the time about *Elza's Story*, I was almost impervious to Paolo Sales, whose manners with his staff ranged from abrupt to abusive. When he did upset me, I would remind myself that this was useful experience for my future which, once the truth came out, was going to be very tough indeed. What I didn't know was that an incurious employee suited him perfectly. He was successful (all the films he'd produced had been low-budget, low-prestige thrillers, and they had all made money) yet he was always conscious of the low opinion in which he was generally held. He was very secretive, always trying to conceal what he was attempting to achieve. In an earlier era he would have employed slaves whose tongues and writing fingers had been excised. But in the present circumstances unquestioning employees like me were the best that could be hoped for.

His last-minute efforts to cut his film's costs meant that he and I stayed in Sydney during the first week of shooting on *Vampire's Gold*. When we arrived at the old goldfields location in Hill End I was curious to see how the film was proceeding. So I went straight to where the filming was taking place.

Fifteen to twenty extras were gathered around a mine shaft at the bottom of which a woman's body had been found. It was still early in the morning but it was already hot and the extras looked tired as they swiped at flies and awaited orders. I began to yawn in sympathy with them. As I watched, a chief of police arrived with his men. The crowd parted to let them through. Then the police withdrew and the crowd regrouped. Then the police arrived again, the crowd parted again, and then there was a slight pause. And then everyone did the same again. Finally the chief of police—after more halts, re-runs and interruptions—moved forward to peer down at the woman's body.

At that stage three figures emerged from the doors of the Hill

End Hotel and began their approach towards the mineshaft. The crowd gawked: these were the town mayor, the local minister and the heroine. The latter was wearing a very striking yellow-and-white striped dress and matching bonnet—something altogether far too grand, I thought, for an ordinary morning on the diggings.

As I watched I also thought that even if I hadn't known Louise, I would have picked her immediately as the heroine. The women extras on the set all moved awkwardly in their dresses—rather as if they were steering large frilly lampshades around—but Louise wore hers as if she'd never worn anything else.

I was starting to feel hot in the morning sun, so I went to the cottage that was serving as the production unit's headquarters to try and settle down to work. I had barely begun when there was a sweeping noise and I looked up to see Louise coming into the room, pulling her long skirts with her. In one hand she held a few creased sheets of paper, looking murderous.

'Where's that bastard, Paolo?' she demanded as she sank into a chair.

'What's the matter?' I replied, adding: 'I thought you looked wonderful. I *was* going to come around and say hello earlier, but I didn't want to distract you.'

She had started to fan herself with the battered sheets of paper. She looked at me, smiled wryly and said she wasn't exactly playing Ophelia—any and all distractions would be welcome. Then the anger returned to her face and she snapped: 'I can't do this, Erika. I should never have agreed to it. Jacquie Paley was right that evening she was going off at me, Paolo Sales *is* a con man, I've been conned!'

She stopped fanning herself and slapped the papers down on the desk in front of me. It was only then I saw that they were pages of the script of *Vampire's Gold*.

'Read that!' Louise ordered.

I read. Catherine, the heroine, leaves her chair by the

fireplace, goes out into the night, hangs around the diggings in the darkness for a while and then the convict-cum-vampire saunters up to join her.

'Why do I go outside?' Louise demanded.

'So you can meet the vampire?' I suggested meekly.

Louise stood up and walked around the room.

'*Exactly*,' she yelled back. 'But granted that Catherine hasn't got second sight and so doesn't know what's in store—*why* does she choose to go outside *then*?'

I watched her as she began pacing again and suddenly I understood what was so distinctive about her appearance. It wasn't that she was much more beautiful than any of the other women in the cast and more glamorously dressed; it was the costume itself. Louise was dressed in just the kind of end-of-the-century Mae West style that *she* had worn in the revue that had made her famous. Nobody, I told myself, could say that we clung to contemporaneity in *Vampire's Gold*. The film, I had learnt already, portrayed a convict being shipped to Australia twenty years after transportation had ceased. Now it featured a heroine dressed in the fashions of four decades after the time when the story was supposed to have occurred.

But Louise was explaining: 'You see, it's not the only time that I get this unaccountable urge to head for the great outdoors. Once or twice, I could cope with. Three times even. But as far as I can see I spend half this movie heading for the door. And for no apparent reason.'

She sat down again, heavily.

'I knew it was a B-grade film, but I thought that the script was going to be halfway competent. When I read the last draft, I said to Paolo: "There's a few things that need to be tightened up here because they don't make sense." And he told me how right I was, and what an intelligent girl I was, and how he was going to have a writer on the set and the minute I had any worries, there would be this writer to sort it out.'

'So,' she continued, 'last week I said, "Where's my writer, eh?"'

And they said the writer is coming up next week with Paolo. So this morning Paolo arrives but he's nowhere to be found and neither is the writer. Well—never mind—all I've got to do is convince the audience that I've got a terrible bladder problem. By the time this movie's been out three months, they'll only have to say, "Louise Riordan!" and everyone will be buzzing for bedpans.'

I smiled at this—and then I froze. *Paolo had said to Louise that there was going to be a writer on the set and then she'd been told that the writer was coming up with Paolo next week.* Understanding dawned. It was exactly the sort of thing Paolo would do. Louise had wanted him to give a job to her friend and Louise had wanted a writer—well, she couldn't complain, could she? He'd done her the favour she had asked for and given her a writer too. After all, one of the reasons he did give for hiring me was that I could write good dialogue.

I turned to Louise, trying to think of how to tell her this. But she had turned away from me and had gone to stand, staring out the cottage window. Her curls had come down around her face and she looked exhausted. I didn't know what to say. For the past few weeks I'd been completely preoccupied by *Elza's Story* and then by the impending end-of-the-world-as-I-knew-it so that the lives of people about me had become like passing traffic in the street. Now I was remembering how kind she had always been to me and how she'd regarded her role in this Paolo Sales film as a means of survival for both of us. I could hear myself saying to Bill King, 'Louise's movie starts next week so at least there will be some cash in the household.'

'Anyway,' said Louise recovering briskly, 'there are compensations. Have you focused vos yeux on my co-star from France?'

'Not in the flesh.'

'The only way to have him. Come here.'

When I joined her at the window I saw a group of the cast walking back towards the set. In the lead was a tall, dark, handsome man wearing a black riding costume and a long black cape. The cape swirled about him as he strode across the summer-browned grass in the bright morning light. He was so attractive that he deserved to be in a picture with twenty times the budget of *Vampire's Gold*.

Anxious to keep the conversation away from the film I asked, 'Oughtn't he take off that cape? He'll pass out in this weather.'

'Etienne knows I love that cape,' said Louise with satisfaction. 'That's why he's wearing it. It's not as hot as it looks, it's silk. I've been trying to persuade wardrobe to sell it to me but they say it's irreplaceable, a real museum piece that was made for some famous tenor to tour India in ... Maybe Paolo could get it for me.'

'Could he do that?'

'It's his movie, isn't it?'

I let her leave without telling her how Paolo had tricked her. I was slowly beginning to realise that Louise's anger about the script arose from something much more substantial than mere exasperation over an incompetently written film. She had had hopes for this project. She had dreamed of converting Catherine, the stock heroine, into a showcase of her particular talents. And it wasn't an unrealistic ambition: in every way the role of Catherine allowed her more scope than did the muted Edwardian lady she had played in her previous picture. This is why the script had to be at least *passable*.

I was confident that all her complaints about the script were true. I had never read it. I had started to do so a few times, but after the first dozen pages I had always given up, bored. Moreover, the script had not seemed very important to me. During the weeks I'd been working with Paolo I'd unconsciously absorbed his attitude towards film-making. His own description of *Vampire's Gold* was that it was (I was so familiar with it that I tended to think of it as one long word) 'a-low-cost-product-with-strong-marketable-elements'.   This meant that the film would be promoted and sold chiefly on the sexual attraction of its stars and the titillation of its vampire-spoof plot. When I remembered how attentively Louise had listened to all my anxieties about *Elza's Story* I felt ashamed of how dismissive I'd been of this project in which she had invested all her hopes of furthering her career.

When I read the script that night it struck me that there was only one good scene in *Vampire's Gold*—but unfortunately Louise did not appear it. This scene was near the start and concerned the vampire's aunt—an elderly baroness from Central Europe who hurriedly sails out to Australia when she discovers that her missing nephew (whom she'd believed drowned at sea) is alive and well and sucking blood on the goldfields of New South Wales. There was much comedy about how she hears this news from the aghast but respectful family solicitor. The Baroness's family had had a vampire streak from way back, but time and careful breeding had diluted it. However (as the aunt often stated) it was 'in zee blood'; and this particular nephew had been especially susceptible because he was the offspring of an unfortunate marriage between close cousins. He'd been carefully watched by his aunt, but he had always been a problem. Eventually he grew tired of the family (especially its rigid vegetarian diet—I liked that touch) and ran away from home to London where—because of his lack of 'papers'—he was apprehended and shipped out to the colony of New South Wales as a convict. On arrival he had escaped and headed for the Hill End goldfields, where because of his handsome dark features and suave Central-European background he was finding it really easy to seduce one colonial gold-digger's wife after another. The role certainly suited Etienne Duprès but apart from this, the script was full of holes. I was particularly worried by a scene in which the vampire was in the hull of the convict ship with all the other prisoners around him. He never thought of going for their throats. 'How could this happen?' I wondered. I thought that the point about vampires was that they needed to suck blood. Then I realised that our vampire could be seasick!

I was so diverted by this idea that for the first time I completely forgot to watch the late-night news bulletins to find out if there had been any developments concerning the screening of *Elza's Story*. If the vampire didn't suck blood on the voyage out because he was seasick, then why didn't he start to do so immediately he had landed?

The answer to this soon appeared. I remembered leafing once through the costume designer's drawings. On land the vampire, like all convicts, had a huge iron ring around his neck. Clearly this would prevent him from getting close enough to a victim to sink his fangs in, I surmised, but once he escaped ... Now, I had the story.

'I did it once,' I said to myself. 'I could do it again. I'll re-read it tonight and I'll talk to Louise. If she agrees, she can pretend to Paolo that they're *her* ideas. He's more likely to listen if he thinks that they come from her.'

But Louise appeared to forget this part of the plan. When she recounted to me the showdown she'd had with Paolo and John Dowell, the director, I noted with alarm that in the exchange, she and I had been turned into a 'we'.

'And I told them,' she reported at frequent intervals, 'that we thought ...'

It was clearly too late to worry about this now and, in any case, she'd won.

As with *Elza's Story*, my first revisions were modest. They might well have remained so except that Louise kept demanding bigger and bigger modifications. She urged me to discard more and more of the original material until soon I was writing whole new scenes only shortly ahead of the filming.

To my amazement, it seemed to work. Louise was so pleased now with the film that her high spirits infected everyone. Even John Dowell started urging me to spoof it up.

'Make it funnier,' he'd say. 'Really go over the top, Erika.'

So Louise, the putative victim, would eye her vampire with starry anticipation as he embraced her with his cape spread wide and his fangs close to her neck.

As it didn't affect the budget, my rewrite was of no interest to Paolo. In any case he appeared to be completely preoccupied with the setting up of his next project. Like Vince Marcus, he would spend all day and most of the night in his office on the phone. As usual he was very secretive about what he was doing; but one rainy night as I was having a drink with Mandy Soames the Production Manager, she said quietly to me, 'He's going big. Big for the next one.'

'I thought he was doing the palm-fringed island thriller,' I answered.

Mandy nodded. 'That too. But he's going to fly. Go big, very big.'

I said nothing, covering my silence by taking a sip of my drink. Mandy was thin and intense with dramatically mascaraed eyes. All day long, she was utterly absorbed in her work. She was businesslike and precise and she never forgot anything. But at night after her fourth whisky she often made pronouncements of the style I've just quoted. I never knew how to respond appropriately. I used to nod gravely, look reflective, wait what seemed a suitable amount of time and then try to steer the conversation back to the mundane.

'Do you think you'll be on Paolo's next film?' I now asked.

'I'll be there,' she said, 'and you'll be there.' She had the wide-eyed stare much practised by young women on the covers of science-fiction paperbacks.

I assumed this wasn't prescience on Mandy's part—it only meant that Paolo Sales had expressed satisfaction with my work. I said nothing. I wouldn't be involved in his next production because the Sydney Film Festival was now approaching. By the time Paolo Sales's next film was in production I would be widely exposed and attacked, sobbing in court and making retribution for rewriting *Elza's Story*.

CHAPTER 11

Although I enjoyed working on *Vampire's Gold*, the best thing about it was that it had—very temporarily—taken my mind off the future. But once February moved into March I knew this brief respite would soon be over. Mid-March was the time when the advance notices for the Sydney Film Festival were to be distributed. On my last day at the Film Board Stuart Cullen had explained to me, at length, how he was intending to use this early publicity as a means of ensuring the screening of *Elza's Story*. His plan was to make the public so curious about the film that if it was withdrawn in response to the Baltic group's protests there would be a general outcry. I'd also read in the newspapers that representatives of the Latvian community were meeting regularly with staff from the Ministry of the Arts—but clearly the Minister himself had decided to put a great distance between himself and the problem. Eisteddfod Sid was now overseas visiting various places of importance ...

With perfect timing, on the fifteenth of the month one of the highly coloured brochures advertising *The Story of the Year of 1912 in the Village of Elza Darzins* arrived in the post for me at the goldfields location. Even though I was certain that the Baltic group would soon see what Stuart Cullen was about and resume their protests, my first sight of that brochure thrilled me. It was real, it was happening, I had done it. There were photographs in the brochure of Elza and her father and the Captain. It was as though I was looking not at characters in a film but at people whom I knew personally. Time and time again I returned to that brochure and studied it with interest. Stuart had written a typically grandiose account of how the screening of *Elza's Story* was an important first for Australia.

With the appearance of the brochure, though, the Baltic group's campaign was remounted with great energy. Every news bulletin, every current affairs show, seemed to include an interview with one of its representatives. One night there was a long newsreel showing Hitler and Stalin signing the 1940 Brest–Litovsk Treaty. The commentator explained that this treaty had given the independent states of Latvia, Estonia and Lithuania to the USSR. His comments continued as the screen now showed soldiers in the street, gunfire, terrified faces of civilians, air attacks and then bare plains, wire fences, prisoners in lines. The blurred black-and-white photography flattened out all the images so that each location merged into the next. This camp was in Latvia: patriots later killed by the Nazis. In Siberia: deportees, many of whom died during resettlement. In Eastern Germany: Balts in slave labour. In West Germany: displaced persons. In Australia: refugees ...

Louise was unimpressed. She came into my room and stood looking critically at the TV screen while an Estonian woman was being interviewed.

The Estonian woman was making a vehement statement about how badly she and her family had been treated on their arrival in Australia and the prejudice that they had faced.

Louise declared, 'They talk about prejudice. Yet here they are protesting about a film that they've never even seen.'

I pointed out that 'they' hadn't had the opportunity. I was about to explain that the film was really only a symbol for the Balts, that what was motivating them was their lost countries and their lost pasts, when she went on:

'In any case, how long do they think that they can go on fighting old wars? All this happened forty years ago!'

I could have told her that *Elza's Story* was similarly about a group of people obsessed by an injustice dating back forty years, but I didn't think Louise would appreciate the irony. The ambivalence I'd felt about the film had returned and it grew as the Baltic group's protests mounted. One minute I would be revelling in the thought of *Elza's Story* being screened, the next minute I'd be wishing that it had never existed—not only because of what might happen to me but also because it was, like these aged Baltic faces on the small screen before me, a reminder of the longevity of wars.

These Latvians, Lithuanians and Estonians were, I realised, still suffering from their defeat in wars imposed upon them. Even though I couldn't disown *Elza's Story*, I almost wished that they could win at least this small battle over its screening—if only to make up for the major battles in which they had never had a chance. In such moods I'd even think of writing to the leaders of the Baltic group to encourage them in their campaign, to tell them how vulnerable Eisteddfod Sid was to hostile publicity. A letter, unsigned, but in Latvian ... that would convince them, surely. 'Attack the Minister fiercely,' I would counsel. 'He is a vain and silly man and will weaken. I am in a position to know this. I am a sympathiser, but I cannot reveal my name. My identity must remain a secret. I am in constant contact with the persons you oppose. Persevere! You are on the brink of victory ...'

Louise was looking at me.

'Do you feel guilty about all this?' she asked.

'A bit.'

'But why should you? You say *Elza's Story* is a great film. Then it should be seen, regardless of the rights and wrongs of Latvia's past!'

I shrugged and remained silent even though I was aware that I ought to tell Louise the truth. But while there was any chance that the screenings could be cancelled I also wanted to keep my secret. That I had done such a thing as a complete rewrite of Balodis's film often seemed unbelievable to me. I would have to remind myself of how *impelled* I'd felt to rewrite *Elza's Story* and how convinced I had been that my version was correct. I knew that I would never be able to convey this feeling to anyone else. Louise would be sure to think I'd been deluded. Yet, perhaps if the film was screened and she saw it ... perhaps she would be impressed before she knew the truth; and then at least she wouldn't think me disgraced, however mad she might otherwise consider me to be.

It strikes me now, though, that if I could have seen the consequences of what I was doing I wouldn't have hesitated to tell her the truth. It's easy enough to present Louise as overbearing—and Louise, always trying to be helpful, was a considerable force to contend with. But I would have been wiser to think more about her affection for me and less about her ways of showing it. For if she was always full of advice and schemes to aid her friends when they were down and out of luck, she also enjoyed their successes more fully and generously than anyone I've ever known. The result of my failure to talk openly to her that evening was that our friendship was undermined. She sensed that something important was being kept from her.

Perhaps that is why, in reaction to my silence, she chose to raise the topic most guaranteed to irritate me.

'Have you asked Paolo yet?'

'What about?' My mind was still fixed on *Elza's Story*.

'About the cape.'

Louise wanted me to ask Paolo Sales to give her the beautiful black cape that Etienne Duprès wore in his vampire role. Her argument was that people are always much more willing to do favours if they're asked by a third party. I wasn't convinced but Louise thought I would make an excellent third party. As she saw it (though she would never have said so to me) she had first got me the job on *Vampire's Gold*. A little friendly assistance from me in a matter so close to her heart didn't seem to her to be unreasonable in the circumstances.

I didn't want to fight with her about the vampire cape. Working on a film-set had taught me the importance of maintaining an appearance of patience, of seeming to be calm and of creating diversions to avoid confrontations. I now looked at her as if I was purely concerned with the practical aspects of the matter.

'But wouldn't it be too long for you, Louise? Etienne's much taller than you are and it comes down to the ground on him. You won't be able to walk in it.'

'I will with my high-heeled boots on. It's just right.'

'You've tried it on?'

'One night in Etienne's room.'

'With your high-heeled boots on?' I was curious.

She nodded.

'And a whip?' I couldn't resist it.

She ignored the remark but frowned. I decided I should return to the subject under discussion.

'Paolo's in a funny mood, Louise. I think it'd be a good idea to postpone all this for a while. You don't want to damage your dealings with him over a cape. I mean there's his next movie to consider.'

'There certainly is,' Louise agreed, switching off the television before going over to stretch herself out on my bed. 'There certainly is his next movie to consider.'

She paused. I turned full around to look at her. She was lying on her side, her hand supporting her head, waiting until she had my complete attention.

'That's why I'm here,' she said. 'I've come to tell you that Paolo is going to produce Jacqueline Paley's movie and that I've got the lead role.'

When Louise announced this news to me I simply stared at her, astounded. It was as though she'd said that Paolo Sales was retiring to a Buddhist monastery and that she and I were going to keep him company.

But Louise was continuing. '*He* wants to produce a classy film. *She* wants someone to produce her classy film. What could be simpler?'

What could be simpler indeed? At last I began to understand.

'You set this up, didn't you?' I asked.

She nodded, proudly. She explained: a few days previously she'd heard that Paolo Sales was having trouble with his big project, the one he'd been spending so much time trying to set up. She'd had the inspiration of getting in contact with Jacqueline and asking her permission to raise the matter of *At Half the Asking* with him.

'I can't believe Jacqueline would agree,' I said. 'This is her great beloved movie and she hates Paolo.'

'It's not much good having a beloved movie that never gets made,' Louise pointed out. 'And she's desperate—it's been going on for a long time, you know ...'

I remembered: like being pregnant, for years.

'... and all her other prospects have fallen through. I explained to her how little Paolo has interfered on *Vampire's Gold*—how we've been allowed to do what we please so long as we stayed within the budget—and that impressed her. So what's happening is that she's coming up here tomorrow—with that planeload of journalists Paolo's flying up to see the shoot.'

'Well,' I said. 'Well, well, well.'

'Of course,' Louise went on, 'it's not definite yet. Paolo's American people have to OK the script, but considering they gave approval to *Vampire's Gold*, I reckon they read not the words but the figures and will let Paolo do as he wishes so long as the money is OK.' She sat up. 'Etienne has to be up at dawn poor darling, so I had to let him sleep, but how about downing a bottle of champagne with me? I am so thrilled about the lead. Jacqueline didn't want me in the role when I auditioned for it last year, but now ...'

We spent the next several hours drinking and discussing *At Half the Asking* with Louise recounting, over and over again, how she had heard about Paolo Sales's setback and how she planned and carried out her coup. Sometime after midnight, drunk and reflective, she announced:

'I think it was meant to happen, you know. When the idea first occurred to me I thought that too much sex with Etienne might be softening my brain, but it seemed such a wonderful opportunity that I knew I couldn't let it pass. I can't spend the rest of my life playing Edwardian older women and vampires' molls ... and when I started thinking about it I found that things started falling easily into place. Things I'd noticed, but not thought about before—like why has Paolo been working so frantically to set up his next project? I realised it just couldn't be his overwhelming ambition. It had to have something to do with the way that the money is arranged—either he gets the next project up and going soon or he loses his American backers. Knowing that gave me leverage. And then when Jacqueline said to me, "What will people say if I ask Paolo Sales to back me after all the times I attacked him?" I answered—and it was as though the words appeared on my tongue—"They'll be very impressed because it will make them realise how committed you are to the project." And every time after that, when either she or Paolo got difficult, it was the same. I felt inspired and utterly confident. Do you think that things are meant to happen?'

In my alcoholic haze I remembered *Elza's Story* and the Tsarist Captain riding into the village.

'I think so,' I said. 'But that doesn't mean,' I went on, 'that you can control the outcome.'

CHAPTER 12

Next morning, suffering the combined effects of alcohol and sleeplessness, I was relieved to discover both Paolo Sales and Mandy were preoccupied with the party of visiting journalists. I stationed myself in a corner of the production office and prayed for the day to be over. From where I was sitting, I could see a panorama of green paddocks, grey bush and faraway blue mountains. Miles and miles and miles of country. I sat staring out the window for some time and then I gave a great yawn. 'Lack of oxygen,' I said to myself and smiled: if there was any shortage of oxygen here, it must be because the planet was running out of it.

My next thought was that it was lack of oxygen in your brain that caused you to yawn. Then I looked up to see Greg Neath, holding a cup of coffee. I was so astonished that all I could do was stare at him in silence.

'Can I join you?'

'How did you—?' Then I recalled: the planeload of journalists from the city. 'Hello,' I said. It seemed like years since we'd met in front of the lifts at the Film Board. 'You're here to see the sights?'

'I've seen them, Erika,' he replied earnestly as he settled his large frame on the seat opposite me, 'and truly wonderful they are too. We took off from Sydney this morning at an hour I hadn't even realised existed and were flown to this mansion with duplex golf courses where we were served something called a Tennessee Breakfast, which seemed to consist mostly of Jack Daniels ... Somebody in this outfit, Erika, has seen far too many movies about hard-drinking journalists. Nonetheless, I felt a whole lot better until I noticed that the pilot and his offsider seemed to be throwing the booze back much faster than the rest of us. Perhaps that was the reason why, on the next leg of the trip, they kept dipping the plane down to show us the local sights. We flew low over several historic villages and a semi-authentic bushranger's cottage and a couple of large lakes and a nectarine orchard ... Have you ever flown low over a nectarine orchard, Erika?'

Somehow he made the prospect sound inviting.

I shook my head, smiling.

'You ought to, though it's like everything else—it's almost over before you're even sure it's happening.'

I started to laugh.

'That's better,' he said. 'You were sitting there looking like Lady Macbeth on an off day. What's the matter? Life with Paolo getting you down?'

I realised that he'd been studying me even though his skew-whiff gaze appeared glazed out of the window, as if fixed on some all too carefully preserved detail of our own historic goldfields. I found the dislocation comforting. He was clearly a person who'd had to go through life with more than his fair share of oddities.

'I feel things are a bit ...' I began, 'I mean, I got into this business by accident and ...'

This rambling sentence was so far removed from all the things that were actually worrying me that I couldn't devise an end to it and came to a halt. Neath must have known that the situation wouldn't be helped by any further probing. He lifted his now empty paper coffee cup and read the inscription on the side: '"Another Pilkington's Paper Product for Big Apple Catering."' Then he said, casually: 'Do you know how I got started in my present career?'

Again I shook my head.

'It wasn't with the intention of becoming the minor figure that I am today in Sydney's film circles,' he began. 'I went to university to become a scientist. Eventually I got a science degree, but by then I'd decided to become a journalist. Few newspapers had any journalists who knew anything about science, so one of them took me on. At the paper they thought that one branch of the sciences was pretty much like another, they also told me to keep my questions short and punchy. One day they sent me to the airport to interview the great man. "Sir Ernest," I asked, "Now that you've split the atom, what are you going to split next?" Well, he took pity on me. He explained in a kindly but incomprehensible fashion that he'd said or done something which had recently caused a big split in the scientific community. I went back to my office and wrote up the story with the headline: "Splitter of Atom Splits Scientists".'

Again I started to laugh. But Neath was continuing:

'The paper was very pleased with me. They took me off science which wasn't important and put me on police rounds which were. My luck held: it was a great time for murders. I spent so much time over at the morgue that they proposed hiring me a desk there. Then, one evening, the Managing Editor found the film critic in a drunken stupor in the lift. It was the opening night of the Film Festival. I saw my chance, I charged in. "Bergman!" I said, "Why, I know him like the back of my hand." They didn't really believe me, but they let me do it. And that's how I became a film reviewer.'

'But you don't write film reviews any more do you?' I asked.

He shook his head. 'I was never very good at it and when my friends started making movies ... Well, it's one thing to criticise a movie made by someone three thousand miles away, but when it's made by one of your friends and they've struggled for ten years to do it ... I got out. Now I just have my column and I edit. Which reminds me, what exactly are you doing for Paolo?'

I said something dismissive about being an offsider, a gofer, a bit of a script assistant.

'Like what?'

I told him the whole story of my revision of *Vampire's Gold* including my favourite addition (the Baroness's embargo on tomatoes for fear they'd put her kin in mind of blood).

At the end, Neath said:

'So you're a scriptdoctor?'

'A scriptdoctor? A scriptdoctor. I don't know.'

I knew the term, but I would never have thought of applying it to myself. At that time the only scriptdoctor I'd ever heard of was an American writer in his late forties whose photograph gave him an immense air of having seen it all, done it all, and been impressed by none of it.

'If that's what you are doing, then that's what you are,' Neath said. 'That's the principle I've always operated on.'

'Perhaps I'm a novice one,' I said, mostly for something to say.

I was thinking how interesting Neath was and how much I liked talking with him.

He looked thoughtful. 'I must admit I've never met a *novice* scriptdoctor before ...' He stopped and smiled at me. 'Perhaps that's the problem. Novice scriptdoctors don't exist. You don't set out to become a scriptdoctor. You don't get trained to be one. You just—there's a word for it—you *manifest*.'

He spread his hands as he spoke. We were both silent, smiling at each other. I was delighted, thinking about *Elza's Story* and realising why I had never found the right word for what I'd done, why it wasn't fraud or forgery or false pretences. My cinematic calling had a name—a name that half suggested veterinary science and half suggested witchcraft. I'd been Peteris Balodis's scriptdoctor.

I was elated. I said, 'I'm very happy to be a scriptdoctor.'

'You look happy,' Neath said. There was a pause. 'Happier,' he added.

'Do you think Paolo will back *At Half the Asking*?' I asked. There was nothing in Neath's manner to suggest he'd noticed me changing topics without preamble, but we both knew that we had reached the point at which Jacqueline Paley and her film had to be mentioned.

'I hope so.' He seemed to hesitate then said, 'Things have been very bad for Jacquie lately because—in addition to the Film Board turning her down—Rita Clarke's book of *At Half the Asking* has just been published. This is upsetting for Jacquie because the intention was to have the book come out in conjunction with the film.'

He explained that Rita Clarke had been contracted by Jacqueline Paley to write the script but that she'd also been given the option of turning it into a novel subsequently. 'Jacquie's taking the publication of the novel as an indication that Rita thinks the movie will never be made. They've fallen out badly over this.'

Knowing Jacqueline's combative character, I guessed that Neath's last comment had been somewhat of an understatement. 'Do you mean they've fallen out terminally?' I asked.

'That's my girl,' he replied.

Only later did it occur to me that he was being deliberately ambiguous.

Louise was in my room again that night, preparing to go out to dinner with Paolo Sales and Jacqueline Paley, drying her hair and putting on the clothes she had brought in for my approval and in the process turning my room into an annexe of her own with all her paraphernalia of jewellery, shoes, credit cards, letters, pages of script, chocolates and wrapping papers.

She was nervous.

'I've never kissed anyone so absentmindedly,' she was saying above the roar of her hairdryer. 'It's one of my biggest passion scenes with Etienne you know, and all those journalists were watching of course, and all I could think about was this meeting with Paolo and Jacquie tonight. What if they don't get on?'

'It's a bit late to worry about that now,' I said unkindly, 'seeing that you and everyone else has known for the last ten years that

they *don't* get on.' But it wasn't Louise's fault that she was marching on to glory while I was probably heading to my downfall,
was it? So I added quickly, 'The simple fact that they're having
this meeting means that they are going to try and get on. So
don't worry about it. They both need this to happen.'

I related what Neath had told me about Jacqueline's break
with Rita Clarke over the publication of Rita's novel. Louise
nodded.

'I've got a copy of the book actually,' she said. 'My agent sent
it up yesterday. I haven't read it yet but if you like I'll drop it in
on my way out.'

I half-hoped she wouldn't remember to deliver Rita Clarke's
novel. But a few minutes later she reappeared on her way out
to dinner with the book in her hand. She came in to me and
kissed me on the forehead. There was a wave of perfume as she
moved.

'You look wonderful. Good luck.'

'I'll call by later if your light is still on.'

Ordinarily, because of my aversion to Rita Clarke, it took
me quite some time to getting around to reading her novels.
Whenever they first appeared I eyed them with ritual hostility.
I'd take them off the shelves in bookshops and survey the price
and the number of pages and the photo of the author, all with
the immediate aim of finding grounds for fault. Then I would
read the opening paragraphs and a random half-page, after
which I would return the volume to its shelf. Then I'd coolly
await the reviews. Any enthusiastic notices I would dismiss as
predictable, but any unfavourable ones I'd store for ammuni-
tion. At a later date—it could be six days or three months—I
would read the novel and dislike it.

Being given the novel of *At Half the Asking* unexpectedly cir-
cumvented all these sensible precautions. When Louise left I
picked the book up and started reading.

I put it down after the first fifteen pages. The heroine irritated
me immediately. She appeared to spend all her time having

deep perceptions about her relationships with her lovers and her children as if their sole purpose for existing was to provide her with this occupation. I supposed that if I had a lover, or children, then I might have found her reflections interesting ... but as it was, all they did was remind me that I'd fallen unrequitedly in love with one man recently and that now I was on the verge of falling in love with another who was Jacqueline Paley's lover! And these were only my private sorrows. In a couple of months, my name would be in the papers and my Latvian mother would be weeping with shame over me.

I put Rita Clarke's novel down on my bedside table and cried myself to sleep.

.

In the middle of the night I woke up to the sound of excited knocking. Louise came in, apologetic but delighted.

'I'm sorry, I'm sorry—but I must tell you, it went marvellously. They just sat and talked as if it was a straightforward business matter. No bitchiness, no recriminations—I could scarcely believe it. I think it's all going to be fine.'

She gave a celebratory twirl on her high heels and then slumped onto my bed. 'I'm so tired I could die.' Then she jumped up again, announced that her shoes were killing her and kicked them off, sending each light sandal in an arc through the air. 'But I'm so excited—I don't think I could sleep.'

'Try,' I said firmly. 'Otherwise you will have bags under your eyes tomorrow and you'll look so awful no-one will ever ask you to act in another film.'

'Quite so,' she said, mimicking me perfectly. 'Quite so.'

At the door, she turned to say goodnight. 'Jacquie was *so* diplomatic. She astonished me. Neath must have been giving her lessons.'

'Perhaps you ought to ask *her* to ask Paolo for the vampire's cape,' I said.

When she'd gone I lay staring at the door. She was so elated that it was impossible for me to be anything but wholeheartedly happy at her good fortune. I picked up the copy of *At Half the Asking* again. As before, the narrator-heroine's continual waves of introspection on the subject of her relationships irritated me, but now Louise and Jacqueline's interest in the script was intriguing enough for me to persevere.

After I'd survived the first few chapters I grudgingly began to understand why they liked it.

CHAPTER 13

The week that followed was frantic. As Louise had suspected, Paolo Sales had to get his next project underway quickly so as to retain the support of his American financiers. Thus work on setting up *At Half the Asking* began immediately, even though shooting was still continuing on *Vampire's Gold* for a few days. Paolo Sales flew off to LA. Mandy and I worked until midnight each day dealing with all the contracts, permits, authorities, exemptions and clearances needed to set up *At Half the Asking*. It was like handling the legal requirements for a fully operational grand duchy or a fair-sized city state. Then disaster struck.

I was walking across the hotel yard on my way from the set to the production cottage when I saw Louise, in costume, rushing towards me, a wardrobe woman hurrying along behind her, calling out to her that she was due on the set, that her gown was getting damp from the grass etc. Louise was ignoring her. The sight was most diverting: a beautiful blonde woman in a full pale blue evening dress with a white towel about her shoulders half concealing a very generous display of cleavage and, behind her, a small severe dark-haired woman, all in white, who was remonstrating fiercely. They both came running towards me through the electricity leads and filming paraphernalia scattered around the hotel looking as incongruous as a pair of Maasai warriors.

When I saw Louise's face I stopped smiling.

'What's the matter?'

'The film is off,' she said, panting. 'Paolo's Americans don't like the script. And to think,' she exclaimed, gesturing at her improbably ornate gown and inches of cleavage, 'they approved *this*.'

'It's the money,' Mandy said when I arrived at the office. She was sitting scrutinising her long red fingernails. If I'd needed any confirmation of Louise's bad news, that would have been sufficient. Mandy was always busy.

Everything had happened during the night. Mandy had been woken by a phone call from Paolo who said that he would be back in a day or two. I knew this meant the collapse of the project. If there'd been any hope of raising finance from any other source Paolo Sales would have stayed in LA.

'It's the money,' Mandy repeated. 'The budget is too big for the risks. First-time writer, first-time director.'

She was permanently unsurprised by developments in the film world and appeared to have neither expectations nor regrets about any particular project. I didn't share her detachment. The news about *At Half the Asking* made me miserable and I kept thinking how desolate not just Louise but Jacqueline Paley herself must be feeling. The fact that there would be relatively little for Mandy and I to do compared to the demands of the previous days made my mood worse. I sat and stared at the dust motes that danced in the shafts of sunlight coming through the production-cottage windows, unable to concentrate on anything bar my own disappointment and the prospect now stretching out before me. I would go back to Sydney shortly to start work not on *At Half the Asking* but on Paolo Sales's next project (I assumed he would revive the palm-fringed island thriller) which I was sure I would despise.

Mandy was looking at me intently with her dramatic, mascaraed eyes.

'*I* think *At Half the Asking* would have made a very good movie,' I began. She didn't disagree, but steered my hostility to where it was due.

'They faxed through the American reader's report,' she said. 'Want to read it?'

The gist of the report was this:

'Narrator, JANE LEWIS, thirty-eightish, leaves her husband, PAUL, and moves with her children LESLEY (girl, ten) and DAVID (nine) to a farm she has bought. Farm is isolated. Local town is small and conservative. Neighbours are unfriendly and suspicious.

'After JANE and her children have been on the farm some months (time periods not clear), a former lover, NIGEL, arrives with his son, NATE (eleven). JANE and NIGEL's attempt to revive their relationship fails. Not clear why. NIGEL returns to the city with NATE, but NATE misses farm and goes back there alone. NATE's parents, NIGEL and CAROLINE, are separated. They discuss whether he can stay on the farm or not. JANE is reluctant as NATE is not easy to control. Asks NIGEL and CAROLINE to come for NATE.

'At farm there are visitors from the city, who smoke marijuana. Local policemen are suspicious. Regard JANE and her friends as radicals and hippies who are likely to make trouble over local conservation issues. They know JANE's farm is losing money. They think they can exploit drug use on the farm to get JANE to leave. They raid the farm, but then the boy, NATE, covers for the adults. Not clear why.

'After this JANE becomes hostile to her city friends. Tells them to leave and not come back. Life on the farm becomes difficult. First there's a drought, then a flood.

'During the flood, CAROLINE comes to retrieve NATE. JANE tells her to wait in the town, JANE tells CAROLINE she'll come to collect her in her four-wheel drive, JANE and NATE and LESLEY and DAVID happily spend the day helping neighbours rescue flood-bound stock. CAROLINE becomes impatient. Thinks floodwaters are dropping, doesn't realise they will rise again with the evening's high tide. Sets off in her own car at dusk and is drowned.

'Starts too slowly. Motivation not established. Not clear why JANE is leaving her husband. Too many speeches. Climax at end (drowning) clichéd. Not enough interest in relationships. Possible interesting area: conflict between values of JANE and her friends and those of small rural community not explored. No potential at present. Advise against.'

As I finished reading I felt a fierce rage on behalf of Louise and of Jacqueline Paley.

In times of tension or conflict, Etienne Duprès had a habit of gazing meaningfully at whoever might be speaking as though only his warm brown eyes could express the depth of his sympathy. At lunch that day his earnest gaze was turned upon me each time I asked to be passed the water or the butter. Louise was sitting silently, scarcely eating, staring ahead. I knew that I should stay away from the topic of *At Half the Asking*, but I was finding that I was unable to do so.

'How did Jacquie take the news?'

Louise shrugged wearily. 'She's in Melbourne. I got Neath. I was going to tell him, but I just didn't have ...' She did not complete her sentence. Etienne patted her hand.

Once again I told myself to leave the topic alone, but still I said:

'I read the assessor's report. It was absurd. Missed the whole point. In fact I'm sure the assessor regards Jane exactly as her husband Paul does. He thinks that she's just this naive restless woman who goes off to the country in pursuit of a dream of pastoral bliss only to discover that real life is more complicated. Cliché, cliché. He completely ignores the real story about the relationship between Jane and Nate. Doesn't even seem to see that. Just goes on about how there's not enough interest in the relationships and how there are too many speeches.'

There was silence. Etienne, who'd been giving me the full support of his unswerving gaze all the time that I'd been speaking, turned his attention to his salad.

'*I* thought there were too many speeches,' said Louise.

I was about to say, 'Not in the book,' when I stopped. I hadn't read the script. As Rita Clarke had written both the script and the novel, it had never occurred to me that they would differ. Like Etienne I started to eat my salad. The day seemed very hot. Too hot to even comment on.

The silence was making Louise uncomfortable.

'I'm sorry I'm so grim. It's just that it was such a good role. They're so ...' She was about to say so rare, so few, but Etienne's warm gaze was now upon her. I guessed her pride reminded her that as he got older, *he* was not going to have a similar problem getting roles even though he had no great talent. She gave his gleaming black head a caress and stood up.

'I don't want to go on about it,' she said to me as we walked towards the caravan that served as her dressing-room.

I ignored her and picked up the script of *At Half the Asking*. She made no comment on this, but settled down at her dressing-table to fix her makeup before filming of a scene from *Vampire's Gold* began.

The caravan was hot. I took the script and went and sat on the doorstep to leaf through it. Two hours later when Louise returned from the filming I was still there.

'The American reader was right after all,' I said to her as I followed her inside the caravan. 'The script missed the story.'

She leant towards the brightly lit mirror, carefully pencilling a line around the edge of her lips. 'What's the story?' she asked.

'Nate and Jane are the story,' I said. 'Especially Nate. His story parallels hers. He runs away from his parents not because he can't get on with them but because he's just like Jane, he wants a new life. That's why, deep down, she's sympathetic, although she doesn't want to acknowledge it. Even when he behaves badly towards her, starts alienating the other children from her and so on, she feels as though she just can't, and shouldn't, get rid of him. She is hurt, she gets confused and depressed, it's just like life with her husband all over again. But when the police come—'

'—Nate steps in,' interrupted Louise. 'And they're reconciled.'

'Which is why,' I added, 'Jane asks Caroline to wait. She is still not sure she wants Nate to leave. And it all ends in tragedy.'

Louise had stopped studying herself in the mirror. I almost knew what she would say before her lips parted.

'You write it,' she said.

'Louise,' I began, gently but firmly, 'Louise, it's too late, the project's off, there's no money. No money, no movie.'

'They didn't like the script,' she continued, ignoring me. 'Other people have known that there's a problem with this script, but you're the first person who has been able to say what's wrong.'

'Louise.'

But she was racing through her plans. She would ring Paolo Sales and tell him to stay in LA. She would get in contact with Jacqueline Paley and get her approval for a rewrite. I would do a revised outline now, tonight, immediately. This would be sent to LA. She seized a tissue and started blotting her lips. Then she was out the door. At the bottom of the caravan steps she stopped abruptly and swung around to look up at me.

'Everyone will agree to everything, Erika. We're all desperate. Don't you realise that? We're all desperate and this is the only chance for any of us.'

I shook my head, half in alarm and half in anticipation. Being a scriptdoctor, I muttered to myself, was getting to be a full-time occupation.

Autumn in Sydney that year was wet. I have a memory of walking out of the apartment into rainy streets and watching the yellowing poplar leaves slowly falling to the damp pavements whenever I paused from working on the script of *At Half the Asking*. Yet, it was *Elza's Story* that was in the back of my mind through all those weeks. I kept up my habit of studying the papers, listening for rumours, trying to establish whether the film would be screened at the Festival or not. The answer was, of course, that no-one knew. I understood the Minister remained under pressure to withdraw the film, but the media seemed to have postponed their interest in the matter: little appeared in the papers except a steady stream of letters with Baltic surnames, all vigorously protesting the occupation of Latvia, Lithuania and Estonia by the USSR. I confess I used to wonder about these letters; although they each appeared under a different name their style and content were so similar that it was easy to imagine they were all written by the same person, whose sense of national outrage had not diminished one iota for forty years and more. For this person, I was sure Latvia could have been annexed yesterday.

Because of my conversation with Neath, however, my concern with the screening of *Elza's Story* now had shifted somewhat. I no longer felt pangs of guilt about my rewrite of the film—obviously being a scriptdoctor was a legitimate occupation—but still at some point I would have to tell Louise (and probably Jacqueline, then Neath) the truth, and seek their help. Yet I hesitated. I'd say to myself that if the film was returned, unscreened, to Moscow, then there was no reason why they, and indeed why anybody, should know. In any case Stuart Cullen, I gathered, was still planning to present a special preview of *Elza's Story* in advance of the Festival. I made up my mind that the perfect time to tell Louise and the others would be immediately after that preview.

When I finally finished my last rewrites to the script of *At Half the Asking*, it was midway through a wet afternoon. I rang Mandy, who immediately sent a courier to collect it. After it was gone, I felt too restless to stay inside and decided to walk around to a photographer's studio where I knew Louise and Etienne were shooting the publicity stills for *Vampire's Gold*. When they were through, we could celebrate by going out for a drink.

Also I had had an idea.

The rain was becoming heavier but I was determined to walk and I arrived at the studio just as the photographic session was coming to an end. Louise, laughing and joking with the photographer, was wearing her anachronistic gold and white striped gown, and Etienne—as I had expected—was resplendent in his vampire's cape. It seemed to me as I watched them move into a pose for one last photo that Louise's face became rather set as I deliberately asked Etienne when he'd be leaving Sydney. I knew he was due to go back to Paris in a matter of days—but I wanted to be sure. I was about to do something for which he might be held responsible.

As Etienne confirmed his departure Louise went away to change. She had a great many encumbrances to remove—petticoats, crinolines, girdles and hairpieces—but Etienne simply slipped out of his cape to reveal ordinary clothes underneath. While we waited for Louise to return he folded the cape into a neat long column and laid it carefully across a chair.

His face filled with consternation when I said I'd come to the studio without a raincoat.

'But it is raining,' he exclaimed. 'You will catch a chill.'

Louise had returned with her costume over her arm. Etienne became so concerned that he seized his own raincoat and advanced towards me with a show that he wouldn't tolerate any protest. I had always imagined France to be full of women who were smart and sophisticated and well-dressed; but, as Etienne with much head-shaking helped me into his coat, I added to all these formidable French ladies of my non- acquaintance a whole population of less fortunate females who died at the first touch of rainwater.

Then I realised his solicitude was a godsend.

It only took seconds, as Etienne was giving his Paris address to the photographer, to pick up the cape and wrap it tightly around my waist. It gave me a pregnancy fore and aft, but under Etienne's large elegant raincoat no-one would notice.

Louise had been watching me. When Etienne turned to her

she closed her eyes and laid her cheek upon his shoulder. 'You need a drink, cherie,' he said tenderly.

'I certainly do,' she said and took his arm and steered him out of the room before he could even think of looking round at where he'd left the cape.

CHAPTER 14

Etienne Duprès was still in Sydney later that week when the preview was held. I have seen *Elza's Story* many times since that decisive silent screening when I began to rewrite it, but it is always the special preview arranged by Stuart Cullen that remains deeply etched in my memory. Even before it started all my prayers about no further screenings of the film seemed to have been answered.

As I was entering the cinema foyer with Louise and Etienne, Ava Markham came up to us with the news. The Soviet embassy in Canberra had apparently become 'alarmed' at the reports of all the Latvian nationalist agitation. Predictably they had withdrawn the film from all the screenings at the Festival. Everyone in the crowded foyer was discussing the ban and there was a great queue waiting to express their sympathies to Stuart Cullen.

'Not that he requires any sympathy,' observed Ava tartly.

I understood what she meant. While the cancellation of the screenings of *Elza's Story* was disastrous for the Film Festival, it was no great loss for Stuart personally. Because of the advance publicity, all the noteworthy guests and local notables were at the film's preview. Consequently nobody of importance was going to miss his victory. He was accepting the general commiserations with considerable grace.

I was doing the same myself. I was saved, and I was getting all I'd ever wanted: one screening, one screening only, of *my* film. I could scarcely believe it. I stood sipping champagne, trying to look serious as people said to me how terrible it was that all the screenings were cancelled. And all the time I was saying to myself as I entered the auditorium: saved, saved, saved.

There was much cheering and clapping as Stuart Cullen climbed on the stage to make a speech. He mentioned my name with warm thanks. Louise leant over to give me a hug. She was wearing a feather boa, determined to be festive in my honour she said, and the feathers went up my nose as she kissed me.

The lights went down in the auditorium and the credits began to roll. Then, far more quickly than I'd expected, Elza was saying the film's opening line:

'In Riga in the winter of 1950 I was reunited with some old friends whom I had not seen for many years.'

My subtitle at the bottom of the screen had no quarrel with this announcement. There they were: the survivors from the village, aged and pinched. (Actually half of them, as the audience would eventually discover, were already dead.) They looked desperately poor, and the grim room in which they were meeting was obviously cold because they were all bundled up in patched coats and covers. Then we were back in the village in 1912 and another meeting—this time of the committee set up to organise the local celebrations for the accession of the Romanovs. Here I started to become tense because my amendments began. The rewrites were small but to me the discrepancy between what I was hearing and what the subtitles read seemed so great that I kept expecting a ripple of consternation to go through the audience each time a disjuncture occurred.

But instead the audience was laughing. A villager with a sideways glance during a royalist speech had conveyed exactly what he thought of the Romanovs. I relaxed slightly but what I was really waiting for was Elza's first philosophical monologue—because here my rewrite had been extreme. I had actually cut half this monologue out and inserted into it elements from a later speech. This made more dramatic sense but had resulted in some notable excisions. Early on in the speech, for example, I'd had to substitute a quote from the famous anarchist, Prince Kropotkin, in place of a reference to Karl Marx. Unfortunately Elza had identified her source. I had a sharp intake of breath as

I heard her say, clear as a bell, 'Karl Marx'.

But the audience was laughing, quietly and not unsympathetically; they seemed to have worked out very quickly that Elza was a touch grandiose.

I relaxed. Then, as the film moved forward to the murder of the schoolteacher, something unexpected happened. I realised for the first time how much people want to accept stories. I began to feel convinced that this audience had moved forward into this film and that if I were now to stand up and announce, 'This isn't real. This is not the film Peteris Balodis made,' they would answer, 'Isn't it? Oh, well, get on with the story.'

There was long applause when the film ended. As we went out to the foyer again I remembered trying to imagine my feelings at this moment. I had expected to be triumphant, gleeful, transported with delight, but I was none of these. It was as though *Elza's Story* had always been meant to exist and that I was merely the agency through which it had made its way into the world. It wasn't mine, it never had been mine.

I would have liked to have slipped away quietly and gone home, but Louise was adamant I should be sociable. Anyone who'd seen us would have thought that she was the one who'd had all the acclaim. Etienne and I simply followed in her wake, nodding and smiling, never branching out on our own—rather as if we were her lord and lady in waiting. Our progress down the foyer was halted at the buffet-table where Neath was standing, watching us approach. Hesitantly I gave him a smile.

The minute Louise saw him, she gave a delighted cry and whirled around. As she whirled, several of her accessories whirled too, with sad results for the buffet-table. She didn't seem to notice.

'You've got your boa in the mousse, Louise.' My voice sounded severe. I was trying to hide the effect Neath's presence was having on me.

Louise let out a peal of laughter. 'Isn't she wonderful?' she demanded of Neath. 'So correct in her precise way. "You've got your boa in the mousse, Louise." She's what I've needed all my life—someone to stop me getting my boas in the mousse!'

I felt myself blushing all the way down my neck. She had imitated my voice perfectly. I laughed because they were all laughing and then, for a diversion, picked up a plate from the table. Etienne was immediately at my side to help me serve myself a completely unwanted supper. He gave encouraging, assiduous little murmurs:

'Ham? The ham looks lovely. Artichokes in vinaigrette? Paté? Yes? And these little Indian savouries. They are different shapes. Ah, these are meat and these are the fish. No fish? You are allergic to it? All seafood? No prawns? What a pity. Some asparagus?'

Etienne was offering me champagne. I accepted, trying to be gracious, and it occurred to me as I was doing so that Etienne's assiduous manners were professional. Once, I thought to myself, once upon a time Etienne Duprès had been a waiter. I knew that there was nothing astonishing about an actor doing time as a waiter, but it seemed to me that this was not the sort of thing I ought to be discovering on this, my night of triumph.

I rejected the seafood but accepted the rest of Etienne's offerings, and was mechanically eating my supper when Bill King appeared. He gave me a big kiss.

'Been working,' he announced apologetically. 'Couldn't get away. Terrible to miss it. Hear they loved it!'

I introduced him to Etienne, explaining that here was the man I'd worked with on the subtitles to *Elza's Story*—but this only made Bill shake his head and interrupt me. 'She did all the work,' he said. 'I was just around to make sure it got on the screen in the right places.'

'It is a great pity,' said Etienne, 'that all Erika's work is now to be wasted.'

'Oh no, I'm sure they'll use her work,' Bill answered. 'Though it does look like it'll be a while before they'll be letting the film out of the country again.'

Etienne, perhaps because he was used to English being the
dominant international language, immediately understood the
implications of what Bill was saying. 'You mean,' he asked, 'that
the Russians will use Erika's English subtitles if the film goes
outside Russia again?'

'Well I don't know what their procedures are,' said Bill easily,
'but why should they do the subtitles all over again when Erika
has already done them so well? I guess they'll get somebody to
check them and then they'll copy them on other prints.'

'So something will come of your hard work after all,' said
Louise.

Bill, Etienne, Louise and Neath were all smiling at me.

I was staring back at them in horror. I had been prepared for
exposure and its consequences in Sydney, but it had never occurred to me that my deception mightn't be discovered until the
film went back to the USSR. I couldn't even begin to speculate
about how long it would take, but I knew what would happen.
A translator would be called in to double-check my subtitles.
Consternation. Perhaps another translator would be called
in. Then the producer and the director themselves would be
alerted. They would listen, disbelievingly. Then Balodis, or
more likely Leblenis, would ring up Somebody Important. The
Somebody Important would then ring up other Somebodies
Important. Moscow would have all its telephone lines jammed.
And eventually somebody would ring Stuart Cullen. Seeking
'clarification' ... Perhaps it would be all over *Pravda*. Maybe
there would be official protests to the Australian Government.

'Of course, it's not the same as having the screenings here.'

Etienne, who thought he'd found the silver lining in this
particular black cloud, must have been disappointed by my silence. I pulled myself together and said well, it was something,
at least. I looked about me desperately. I wanted to get away
from them and recover. It seemed that the only safe place to be
after a crisis with *Elza's Story* was a toilet cubicle.

But there was no way of escaping now. I was just standing

there before the buffet staring at them and holding my plate. I had to grip it tightly because my hands had begun to tremble as I turned to place it on the table. The prawns which Etienne had been admiring formed a pink mound. I reached out and spooned a load of them and began to eat them with a studied determination. I didn't like the taste so I smothered them with cocktail sauce. I began to feel quite calm as I ate.

I was sick for eleven days. Twice during that time when I thought I might be recovering, I pulled myself shakily out of bed and went to the local delicatessen where I bought a tin of crabmeat. I can remember very clearly going off to buy that crabmeat and eating it afterwards, seated on the side of the bath, because even the faint seawater odour of the bland tinned crab made me queasy—but I have noticed that I never mentioned buying the crabmeat in my diary. This is interesting, because otherwise my account of those days is obsessively detailed. I recorded every time Louise came in to ask me how I was feeling and noted my irritation with her visits. I wanted to be left alone. I didn't want her kindly concern. I was bored by having to invent, for her benefit, accounts of consultations with the neighbourhood's doctor. I knew any doctor would diagnose my retching and fever and fiery skin as severe allergic reaction. In my diary I noted my relief when, at the end of the week following the preview screening of *Elza's Story*, Louise began working on *At Half the Asking*. Now she could only come in to enquire after my health when she returned home in the evening.

Most of the diary entries are concerned with one thing: the discovery of my rewrite of *Elza's Story*. When would that occur? My entries had a strong ring of grievance about them. Many times I pointed out to myself that I had done something foolish and dangerous in unilaterally appointing myself Peteris Balodis's scriptdoctor; I accepted that I was going to be, and that

I deserved to be, punished for this. But I also wanted the USSR and Balodis and Leblenis to uncover me and denounce me and get it all over and done with in the least possible delay. This was now my second great period of fear and suspense over the scriptdoctoring of *Elza's Story*. I was getting weary of waiting to be found out.

In my diary I wrote laboriously plotted accounts of various scenarios of how my rewrite would be discovered, and how long this might take—with projections as to dates in the margins. The simplest scenario was that Balodis or Leblenis or one of their close associates spoke English and that—out of sheer interest—they decided to check the subtitles of the film on its return to Moscow. This would result in my rapid exposure. But there were various complications: Balodis and Leblenis might not speak English or know anyone who did, they might be away from Moscow when the film was returned, they might not have easy access to the print or opportunities to screen it ... All my experiences with the Soviet consulate came into play here as I thought of the infinite variety of bureaucratic obstructions that the Russians could devise to delay my exposure and punishment.

The more complicated scenario was that it would only occur to Balodis and Leblenis to check the subtitles when they began to notice something odd in the story of the film as recounted in the reviews of the critics who'd seen it at its Sydney preview. But this was clearly going to take some time. The reviews would have to be forwarded to the USSR, and translated; and even then the film-makers might easily ascribe any strange discrepancies to the vagaries of translation, or else to the possibility that some critics on a first viewing of their long and complex film had either misunderstood it or become confused. It seemed to me that it might require a whole accumulation of translated reviews from Sydney before Balodis and Leblenis began to suspect that their film as screened was substantially different in its story from the one they had made.

And how long would that take? I might be in this stalemate for months. My diary records hours and hours of exasperation as I railed against the Russians who, it seemed to me, were now clearly the villains in the case. They had sent the film abroad under such circumstances as to maximise the chances of trouble occurring—first by sending the Latvian-language version of the film to Sydney and secondly by hedging its translation with such ridiculous conditions. And now they were not even doing me the courtesy of letting me know my fate.

Soon, however, I found another object for my sense of grievance, one much closer to home.

I had begun to take offence at the fact that Louise was paying me less attention. As this was exactly what I wished her to do, my reaction was illogical—but I was in no state of mind for consistency and, in any case, I held her partly responsible for my plight because it was at her urgings in the first place that I'd applied for the Film Board position. My diary entries register that she seemed preoccupied. There were quick phone calls, sudden late-night departures, early-morning returns and a man's voice at the door delivering her home at dawn. She had acquired a new lover.

I wasn't surprised by the speed with which she had replaced Etienne, who'd left for Paris just after the preview, but at her secrecy. I was used to hearing about Louise's lovers and, as she liked sleeping in her own bed, also to meeting them at breakfast. It didn't occur to me that perhaps she thought it was inappropriate to bring her new lover home when I was apparently very ill.

I could simply have asked her who she was seeing, but I never did. I wrote in the diary that I was very relieved not to have another of her grand passionate affairs flourishing under my nose when I was in this state of crisis with the USSR.

But anxiety was making me sleep poorly. Inevitably early one morning I distinctly heard the voice of Louise's lover as he said goodbye to her at the door. I recognised it immediately.

I was shaken with anger and a deep sense of betrayal. I pretended that I was asleep when she put her head into my room to say hello, but I spent the rest of the day waiting for her to come home again and preparing my lines:

'Well, well, well,' I'd say to her to begin with, 'a genuine old-fashioned clandestine affair. I didn't think people had them any more.'

I didn't get a chance to deliver that line. When she came in that evening the first thing she said was: 'Bill King was asking after you today. I'm sure he thinks you're pregnant, but he didn't quite know how to ask. Just shifted from one foot to the other ...' she acted out his performance '... and looked embarrassed.'

'Tell him I am,' I said.

She looked at me. 'Are you?'

I shrugged. 'What does it matter? Tell him I'm having triplets. Tell him soap operas are right.'

'What do you mean?'

'I mean that soap operas are accurate in their depiction of life, Louise. They're spot on. They show us life exactly as it is.'

I could see her confusion and I was preparing to deliver my line when she said, 'Look, I don't know what you're on about or why you are so hostile, but I assume that I've offended you in some way. I don't know how and I think you ought to tell me because, as you know, shooting starts in a fortnight and I'm really too busy to take part in strange little scenes like this one.'

'But not too busy to see Neath every night?'

She didn't answer this. I could feel my face flushing with anger, but knew too that I could be in tears in a minute. So I went on:

'He must be leading a very full life, our nice friend Neath. Keeping two demanding women like you and Jacqueline happy.'

Again she said nothing, she was staring straight at me.

'Perhaps you don't remember Jacqueline?' I continued. This was elaborate sarcasm as they were working together each day. 'Or maybe you just don't feel guilty about her even though you manipulated her to make her film so that you could win the lead role. And now you've got her boyfriend as a bonus.'

It turned out though that I had picked exactly the wrong person in Jacqueline. I had left Louise totally with the advantage.

'Oh I do remember Jacqueline,' she said to me, in perfect mimicry of my voice. 'And so does Neath. And for your information, Erika, I've only been seeing him since Jacquie Paley started spending her nights with Paolo Sales.'

Louise told me afterwards that on that occasion she had passed up the opportunity for one of the great exits of her life.

'A real sacrifice for an actress,' she commented. 'But you were looking so shocked and crestfallen that I felt sorry for you.'

So instead she stayed and said quite gently:

'That sort of thing often happens when people are working closely together on pictures. It can be very demanding and emotional. Like wartime.'

Later I used to think that it was typical of me to displace my own feelings of hurt and jealousy onto Jacqueline and to pretend that my concern was solely for her, but at least that fight with Louise was cathartic. It gave me the stimulus to lift myself out of my self-imposed illness. I suddenly realised that I was doing no real service to anybody, especially myself, lying in bed—hoping, in my more depressed moments, to slide into death to relieve my family of the shame of my crime and punishment, but, at the same time, not really wanting to die. The next morning I rang Mandy Soames to ensure there was still a production job open for me in the making of *At Half the Asking*. Shortly afterwards I went back to work.

The following months I recall indistinctly. The days were very long and busy, packed with the demands and urgencies of making *At Half the Asking*; my accounts of that time in my diary were fragmentary. Actually, I rarely wrote in it because when I wasn't working, I spent all my time with Mandy and the other crew. I now regarded my period of self-imposed illness as an aberration. I realised that my preoccupation with being denounced by the USSR was more a reflection of my state of mind than the reality of the situation because in all my scenarios about exposure by Moscow there had been one fundamental flaw: it was highly probable that Balodis would *never* learn about the reception that his film had received in Sydney. It was not in the interests of anyone in authority in the Soviet Union that he should know that it had been hailed as a masterpiece abroad, so it was unlikely that he would ever get to see enough reviews of the film as screened in Sydney to realise that something strange had happened to *Elza's Story*.

I thought that I was free now to proceed with my own life. If you had asked me at the time I would have said that I was very busy and quite content; my major interest had become the scheme Louise and I had hatched to have me included in the publicity team being set up by Paolo to promote *At Half the Asking* overseas. In truth I didn't want the production of *At Half the Asking* to finish at all: hence my enthusiasm for joining the publicity team. Louise had said, rightly, that making films can be like wartime. There was always excitement, desperation, joint purpose and camaraderie during the filming of *At Half the Asking*.

Once it was decided that I would be part of the promotions team, I spent long hours with Paolo while he plotted his strategy. We would go to Cannes in the spring, and from there around the world. Editing was now going smoothly, and Paolo was convinced the film would be a great success.

This plan had an extra attraction for me: I had learnt that the film Vince Marcus had made in Hollywood would also be going to Cannes.

Yet it's obvious to me now that all this excessive work and socialising was as abnormal as my retreat into illness had been ... because it was during those months that I slowly came to realise what was to be the fate of *Elza's Story*. The Soviet authorities would now regard the whole matter of the film called *The Story of the Year of 1912 in the Village of Elza Darzins* as a series of errors from the date of its production to the time of its one and only screening in faraway Australia. As a result, all prints of it, including the one which had gone on its long journey to Sydney, would be destroyed or be officially misfiled or mislaid, deliberately forgotten, until doubts could be passed as to the very existence of the film itself.

As for me, I was of no importance. Who would believe me if I told them the truth; and even if they did, how could I ever prove it? Nobody would ever bother to denounce me. I was even less of an issue than the film that was about to disappear.

I now knew Moscow's retribution. All my work had been wasted. I was living with a loss. They had taken *Elza's Story* away.

PART THREE

ZOLITE

ENLIGHTENED SYSTEM

SIR: The assertion that in a Latvian card game Queens are rated higher than Kings is but a trivial example of the high esteem accorded to women in Latvian folklore ... In the independent Latvian republic between the wars women enjoyed complete equality. It came as a shock to Latvian migrants in the late 1940s that a similar equality did not exist then in Australia.

A Bicevskis

(from the correspondence columns of the *Sydney Morning Herald*)

CHAPTER 15

I liked the South of France. I hadn't expected to. I had thought of it merely as a backdrop to the famous Film Festival: tourists, beaches, starlets and millionaires; gaudy, expensive and over-patronised. But in the car from the airport I was already preoccupied with trying to find a simile for the blue of the sea. The others soon began to complain: Paolo Sales about the Festival arrangements, Jacqueline Paley about the prices, Mandy about the accommodation, but this was *my* first foreign country and everything intrigued me. I stood at the window of the small and noisy hotel room I shared with Louise, staring out with delight. I was eager to explore. I wasn't deterred by Cannes' crowded streets because even while I was fighting my way through them I didn't regard the crowds as real—more like extras on a film set. Any minute now someone was going to come out with a hailer and shout directions: approach the cameras slowly, don't bunch up in the middle, keep it steady, OK, OK, that's much better. Can we have it once again, please, ladies and gentlemen?

Before I arrived, I hadn't anticipated having any time to sightsee, but the first news we had received upon landing was that Paolo Sales's American backers had taken control of *At Half the Asking*. They had decided that *they* could sell the film more effectively and so, while we were on the plane from Sydney, they had made arrangements so that neither Paolo nor Jacqueline was any longer in charge of its international marketing and promotion. There had always been an American co-producer overseeing the project; now, he told us upon our arrival, he'd be our 'frontline' man.

As a result the whole Australian entourage of *At Half the*

Asking behaved in Cannes like the vanguard of a conquering army turned suddenly into a government-in-exile. The phones rang in another suite, our American co-producer taking all the calls. After our initial, brief meeting we never saw him. I was reminded of the always invisible cast that Vince Marcus dealt with on his phone: the top studio executives, the great producers, the world-famous stars, the box-office winners, 'Berlitz, Forrest, Summers and Jack'. On their elevated plane, these amazing and powerful beings oscillated between their yachts in the harbour and their villas in the hills. There was nothing Paolo and Jacqueline could do but try to conceal the extent of their downfall while in public—and sit, privately morose, attempting to second-guess developments and plot their future strategy. Meanwhile Louise and I ended up with paid holidays.

Louise spent her time with Neath (who was covering the Festival for his paper) but I travelled up into the hills or down the coast to the Italian frontier on day trips. In the evenings I received detailed bulletins from Louise: Stuart Cullen had arrived in town and had been overheard expounding in a restaurant; she had met Vince Marcus and told me that she had been invited to the premiere of his film and a reception afterwards.

'You must come too,' she said.

'But I haven't been invited,' I replied.

Louise knew of my interest in Vince, but she didn't know the terms on which we had parted.

'We'll see about that,' she said firmly.

She kept insisting, but I shied away from the topic. I wasn't even sure that Vince would remember me.

As the premiere approached, however, I couldn't stop thinking about it. The night before, I was unable to sleep. I tossed for several hours and finally at dawn, rose and dressed and went down to the Promenade. Cannes seemed almost eerie after the crowds of the day. I started to walk along the seafront watching the morning light coming through low clouds which turned pink then gold. The sea went through several shifts of light and shadows as the sun began to rise slowly over the horizon. It occurred to me that what I felt about Cannes and the South of France was just like what I'd felt about the two men to whom I'd been attracted: we would have gotten on just fine if the world could have retreated for a while and let us get to know each other ... But then it also occurred to me that this thought summed up my history perfectly. It was typical that I should come to this conclusion about Cannes and the South of France in the middle of its most populous week.

Behind me the morning's bustle was starting. On the way back to the hotel I stopped to buy a paper. The tobacconist's counter was full of glossy papers and magazines covering the Festival. I was glancing at them to assure myself that there was nothing of interest to me when my gaze was suddenly attracted to a headline halfway down the crowded front page of the early-morning edition of *Release*.

'Canned Lats for Cannes?' it asked.

In smaller type underneath there was a further enquiry: 'Soviet Shelf Job Release?'

The article was written in that abbreviated allusive film-press style which always suggested to me that film journalists wrote for the benefit of one specific reader rather than for general distribution. But after I'd deciphered the sentences, there it was. The organisers of the Cannes Film Festival were expecting to be informed early this morning whether or not the Soviet authorities were going to enter the previously suppressed film *Elza's Story* (*The Story of the Year of 1912 in the Village of Elza Darzins*) in the Festival instead of the announced entry *Games for Sasha and Myra* (directed by A Dashkov).

That was it. Otherwise there was a marked lack of information in the article. It wound up with an account of a similar incident which had taken place in 1969 when Tarkovsky's *Andrei Rublev* was screened at the Cannes Film Festival amidst much confusion and after forty minutes of film had been shorn from the print—apparently at the last moment.

I noted that there were no references to recent screenings of *Elza's Story* outside the USSR. There was nothing in the article to suggest that anything strange had taken place on the previous and only occasion when *Elza's Story* had been screened twelve months before in Sydney. There were no mentions of any problems with the translation or of any oddities in the subtitling. I told myself that it was extremely unlikely that the print of the film that was coming to Cannes would be the one with my subtitles ... but my heart started beating fast. I kept thinking that clearly the decision to release the film was being made at the last minute. What could be more reasonable to assume than that the Russians would seize the reels of the one and only print of *Elza's Story* that had ever been outside the USSR and send them on the next flight west?

Everything that I had dreaded as a possibility at the Sydney Film Festival now could occur—at another, more famous, film festival on the other side of the world.

I hurried to the Festival Information Centre. There, at least, I would be able to ask for the latest details. But as I waited in the long queue it occurred to me that I had no idea of how to ask for the information I wanted. The questions I really needed to have answered were: 'Is the film *The Story of the Year of 1912 in the Village of Elza Darzins* definitely going to be shown at the Festival? If so, will it be shown with English subtitles? If so, what is the name of the translator?' But even to me this sounded like the final series of questions at an international film trivia quiz contest. I could just as easily ask the counter attendant: 'What was the date of the Treaty which concluded the First Opium War, where was it signed and by what representatives of which governments?'

I was still pondering this problem when I finally reached the counter. I blurted out in my broken French:

'Excuse me—can you tell me what language the Latvian film, *Elza's Story*, is in?'

The counter attendant gave me an authoritative stare. Her answer came back very promptly.

'Latvian.'

Ah yes, I cursed myself mentally. But I could use another method to find out what I now so desperately needed to know. So I asked, in English this time:

'I thought it might be dubbed into Russian?'

I was given another stare, but this time it contained more respect. The counter attendant left her position to hold conference with a colleague who appeared to be in charge. Throughout their rapid conversation in French I could only identify the constant repetition of the word 'Russie'. The attendant took a long time to return. When she did, she said, using the most impeccably spoken and official English:

'We understand that dubbing into Russian is the usual practice, but we also understand that the usual practice has not been followed in this instance.'

After that I began to despair. From the conversation it was quite clear that the film *was* going to be shown; what was worse, it was also quite clear that it would be shown in Latvian. I knew that I was incapable of doing anything except to obsessively wait for more news of *Elza's Story*.

I sat in a corner of the Information Centre and just waited and, from time to time, I remembered that it had all begun like this. Me, waiting interminably in the corridor of the State Film Board in Sydney, me and my imaginary Latvian great-grandmother; and then, late in the afternoon, I learnt the film would be screened at eleven o'clock the next day.

I gathered myself up. I didn't have the strength, or the nerve, to ask any further questions. I went back to the hotel room. It was filled with the mayhem of Louise's possessions.

I lay down on my bed. I had been awake for thirty-six hours, but I knew that I wasn't going to sleep. I folded my arms under my head and stared at the ceiling.

CHAPTER 16

I was still lying in that position two hours later when Louise returned. I heard the bustle in the corridor well before she put the key in the door. I thought of feigning sleep, but then I glanced at her as she came into the room and said a brief hello. I wasn't going to begin a conversation. I had more important things to worry about.

Her arms were full. Amongst many other things she carried a great bouquet of red-gold rosebuds. She paused and gave a kick and then another kick. Two delicate gold sandals with slender high heels did somersaults in the air and landed soundlessly on the thick carpet. Meanwhile she was bundling things onto her bed: parcels, newspapers, flowers, programs, brochures. In the impact several of the lighter bits of paper sprayed off the bed and scattered onto the floor.

But Louise didn't notice. She picked up the bouquet and exclaimed, 'Scissors, scissors!'

I didn't reply. I had seen dozens of Louise's entrances. Once I would have stopped whatever I was doing and admired the roses and found the scissors. Now I merely watched.

I was thinking that I should have expected this: one of the actress-in-solo-with-a-bouquet performances. I was still watching when she dropped the scissors, bent down to retrieve them and picked up something else from the litter of papers lying on the floor. She handed it to me and then proceeded with the bouquet, humming happily to herself.

It was a brightly coloured Festival brochure of the type used to advertise special screenings. Across the top in large letters was '*L'Histoire d'Elze—Latvie*'. Without uttering a word I began to read. There were screening times for the film announced in four languages. Below these was a paragraph in each language about the film, but I immediately stopped reading the English paragraph when halfway through I noticed one small phrase in very small print at the very bottom of the page.

'French subtitles only.'

French subtitles only! My heart leapt. Of course! Why hadn't I thought of that? That was the simple question I had needed to ask the counter attendant: in what language are the subtitles?

When I looked over at Louise she was still humming. For the first time since she had come into the room I smiled at her.

I felt like celebrating. 'I'll order us something to drink,' I said, jumping from the bed.

Louise was too good an actress to acknowledge my sudden change of mood. But I saw her turn to watch as I folded the brochure about *L'Histoire d'Elze* into a paper plane. Then I took it to the window and sent it off—in what I hoped was the direction of the USSR.

I didn't stay to watch its flight. I rang room service and ordered Russian caviar and French champagne and then, as Louise continued to watch, now in open amazement, I tidied the room.

·

I can recall practically nothing of the rest of that afternoon, which is understandable as I drank glass after glass of champagne on a virtually empty stomach after a sleepless night. Louise, who wasn't much more sober than I was, decided to skip the premiere of Vince's film; but she was still determined to go to the reception and to take me with her. When the time came to leave I tried to remonstrate with her one last time. I gestured at my blouse and slacks and said:

'I won't be allowed in, Louise. It's a *gala* reception, you said so yourself, a very *formal* evening, by invitation only. Even if I was capable of getting dressed I don't have anything grand enough to wear.'

But Louise was prepared for this. She leapt up and from her case she drew out something black, the vampire cape. She shook it and patted it and placed it carefully over her arm.

'Tonight is *your* turn to wear it,' she said.

She then pushed me into the shower, cajoled me into my best dress and organised my hair while obliging me to drink two cups of black coffee.

I was tired. On the way to the reception I was glad to be able to rest my head against the soft velour seat of our taxi and close my eyes. It wasn't until we had actually reached our destination that I opened them again. What I saw then, however, confirmed my worst fears. For once, I told myself, Louise had gone too far. This was the one caper that was bound to fail.

There was an attendant, in black tie, positioned at the kerb. Directly above him, at the top of a flight of steps, a couple in full evening dress were being ushered into the lit-up building through rows of doormen and security guards. On the door as it closed silently behind them I could read a large notice stating '*Entrée Interdite Sauf Invitation*'. I didn't need a translator.

I turned to Louise, 'Look!' I wailed. 'They won't let me in, I told you ... I don't have an invitation.'

She remained unperturbed. 'This will solve the problem,' she said as she unfolded the cape from her arm. 'We are wearing this.'

Then she proceeded to slip it on. I looked at her and asked, bewildered:

'Simultaneously?'

'Pay the man,' was all she deigned to reply.

As I handed over the money she began to explain. 'There,' she pointed out the cab window, 'is the party.' Her finger indicated the second floor of the building, from which came most of the lights. She continued: 'I was here a few days ago.' She ruffled her hair as she spoke, slowly, making sure I would follow her every word. 'I know this place. At the back it overlooks a lane, which is directly below the ladies' lounge—'

'What are you doing?' I interrupted. Her detailed description sounded to me as if we were terrorists planning an assault. 'We're not *raiding* this place, are we?'

She merely lifted her chin. 'I shall walk up these stairs in a moment, Erika, in this cape, and I shall show my invitation, and I shall enter. You will walk around to the back of the building, and into the lane. When I am inside I shall go to the ladies' lounge, and through a window I shall throw you—'

'Vince?'

'The cape. And inside, in a pocket, you will find the invitation. You will then put the cape on, you will walk up these steps ...'

As she was speaking she opened the cab door and stepped out. She walked haughtily up the stairs, the cape swirling from her shoulders, her chin high, her hair light gold on her shoulders. The taxi driver and I watched her going inside as the attendants respectfully opened the doors. When I was closing the taxi door, the driver looked around at me enquiringly. I wasn't sure of his command of English, but some comment seemed necessary.

'This isn't how I imagined it,' I said.

It all went exactly as planned. I crossed the footpath and hurried down the side lane, but Louise had neglected to mention that all the service entries to the building also led onto that lane. Rather than skulking alone in the shadows, I was thus the object of the gazes of a number of cleaners and waiters who'd stepped outside for a cigarette, of porters arriving for the night shift and of the drivers of several delivery vans. I located the appointed window, praying that Louise would hurry while trying to convey an impression of ladylike insouciance. I had just moved out of the way of a laundry van when I heard a laugh above me. Louise, a glass of champagne in one hand and the cape in the other, was hanging perilously over the window sill. I stepped forward and she laughed again and let the cape fall. For a minute it fanned out black in the air and seemed too large to catch—then I'd gathered it in my arms. I slipped it on. My audience of cleaners, waiters, porters and deliverers eyed me in silence over their cigarettes without displaying the slightest evidence of surprise or curiosity.

The party occupied two large reception rooms, both of which led onto a wide balcony. The second room had a dance floor with tables around it, but most of the guests were in the first room so that I had to ease my way through the crowd while I looked for Louise. On my way in I'd had a fantasy that she'd be chatting with Vince and they would turn to me when I came up to them and his eyes would widen in surprise then delight. But when I finally found her, she was with Stuart Cullen.

Stuart greeted me exactly as if he had seen me earlier that day in the corridors of the State Film Board in Sydney. Then continued to talk in his usual long, sweeping sentences ... They passed by me like huge expanses of landscapes, the American prairies or the Russian steppes perhaps, while I attempted to semaphore a question to Louise. At last a waiter provided me with an intermission. Louise managed to glance at me and say casually:

'Oh, have you come across Vince yet? He was down the end of the other room by the dance floor and I was meaning to go down and congratulate him on his film, apparently it's had a great reception.'

I would have extricated myself then, but Stuart was saying to me:

'You've heard the news about *Elza's Story* of course?'

I nodded.

'It really has taken me almost the full twelve months to get the Soviet authorities to see the events that happened in Sydney in their full perspective,' he said.

I froze. I was too dumbfounded to do any more than stare at him, scarcely knowing what to think. Had I been discovered? Had the rewrite been hushed up? But he was proceeding on imperturbably.

'There were, inevitably, people at all levels of the bureaucracy who were inclined to consider that the relatively small hostile nationalistic response in Sydney was a reason to prevent all further steps towards the international distribution of the film, but I did manage to convince them that a similar response was most unlikely to occur in the context of the Cannes Festival, and that in view of the enthusiastic reception it had met with in Sydney, it would be most unwise not to take advantage of the opportunities it presented for the promotion of Soviet films in a year when, to be candid, most of the output has been undistinguished.'

Stuart was prevented by the crowd surrounding us from taking one of his characteristic turns about the room, but his mode of address seemed to me to be even more grandly statesmanlike than usual. It struck me that he too was a bit drunk. This had not affected his grasp of events, however, because with scarcely a pause he then leaned forward and confided to me:

'I regret to say, however, Erika, that given the ebb and flow of political influence within the Soviet film bureaucracy it would be optimistic to expect that the pressure necessary to ensure the film's proper international promotion will be maintained.'

After this communication, I could scarcely come out with some ill-informed and honest remark like: 'I didn't know you'd been in Moscow.' I was trying to phrase a question appropriate to a figure of his importance when Louise butted in to exclaim with great fervour:

'I'm so hungry—isn't there a buffet around here somewhere?'

As she spoke, she laid her hand on Stuart's arm, clearly to indicate to him that he was expected to accompany her to the buffet—but at the same time she gave me a look which told me that I ought to be attending to the night's real business. There was no way I could convey to her that I was, in fact, eager to hear every possible detail of Stuart's recent visit to the USSR. So I had to smile graciously and watch, in frustration, while she led him away. I consoled myself with the thought that by the next time I met Stuart, I'd have a question prepared through which I might locate, somewhere in one of his Byzantine sentences, the fate of my rewrite of *Elza's Story*.

But it was also occurring to me that he could not have talked as he had of *Elza's Story* and its eventual progress out into the world if there had been a shadow of doubt over it, if there'd been any slight murmur arising from its first screening outside the USSR. From his massive confidence I could only deduce there had been nothing. Either my rewrite had never been discovered—or else it *had* been ... and had been dismissed. Either way it had disappeared. The only form in which it now existed was in my vivid memory of its one screening in Sydney. From now on all recollections of it would be blurred, forgotten and lost.

I realised I had to compose myself. In my cape I looked brave. Also conspicuous. Neither of which suited me. Actually I wanted to run away—so I did what I had done once before in Sydney when Stuart had brought bad news.

I retired to the Ladies'.

As soon as I entered I realised why Louise had had such a clear memory of the place. Up on one wall of the room rose an utterly impractical-looking wrought iron staircase leading to a narrow mezzanine. The whole room looked as if it had strayed from the set of an operetta. In the middle of the mezzanine level was a large window. I could imagine the scene: Louise sweeping into the room in her black cape, past the women at the mirrors and washbasins, past the women coming out of the cubicles, up the stairs and towards the window ... causing some flurry and consternation, was she going to jump? Then, with a flourish, throwing her cape out into the night, and passing by again just as mysteriously.

It was just too good a scene. I began to laugh and immediately cheered up. I checked my appearance in a mirror: the cape *did* suit me rather well, I thought.

So I went out, feeling ready now to be brave and conspicuous.

Yet my entry into the main room did not live up to my expectations. I sidled in and eyed my surroundings from the cover of a large floral arrangement. The dancing seemed to be over for the night, but there were still groups of people seated at tables around the walls. At one of these tables at the far end, I saw Vince. He was facing me, but his eyes were fixed upon another man who was addressing him with much gesticulation. I accepted a drink from a passing waiter and eased my way to the French doors and onto the balcony.

From there I could watch the room.

The group around Vince was thinning. The man talking to him was leaving now. The man moved away from the table waving goodnight; I stood watching, and then, at Vince's table, a woman stood up. She was pretty with dark wavy hair, her long dress was a brilliant red with gold flowers. Now she stood by his chair, leaning forward to talk to him. He laughed at something she said and she gave him a kiss on the cheek. Then they each said something to the other and then they both laughed and then she seated herself on his lap.

I looked away and then looked again. She was still sitting on his knee. He had his arm about her.

'Well, that's that,' I muttered to myself.

I retreated to the other end of balcony where I stood, my cheeks warm, thinking that this was surely my life. I would never mistake it for any other. If I were to get amnesia and the doctors were to describe to me a number of lives which could possibly have been mine, I would be able to identify my own without a moment's hesitation.

I knew that Louise would soon come looking for me. She would go into the main room to check my progress with Vince and then set out to find me. I supposed I ought to save her the trouble, but I was incapable of moving. The memory of her stratagems on my behalf depressed me. It occurred to me that while I'd always thought I was cautious, I had been as romantic about my relationship with Louise as I had been about my imagined reunion with Vince. I'd been charmed by our alliance, thinking that she and I could get by with each other's aid and now it seemed as though we'd been playing games, pretending we could influence events, and jointly leading ourselves into ever greater absurdities. This evening was typical. Instead of escapades involving capes and back lanes, we would have been better off doing some prior research and establishing that Vince was unattached.

'What's happening?' Sure enough, within a minute or two she was by my side.

For an answer I touched her arm and drew her to the French doors. The situation at the table had not altered. Vince still had the dark-haired woman seated on his knee. Louise eyed her briefly and said: 'Her? She's no-one of any importance. Have you spoken to him?'

I shook my head.

'Well, now's your chance,' she said dryly as the dark-haired woman rose from Vince's lap and made her way up the room in the direction of the buffet.

'You mean take over while she's gone?'

She nodded. 'He's a big boy. He can make up his own mind.'

I wasn't given the opportunity to discuss the matter further because she actually propelled me forward into the room. Vince was now in profile to me, listening to what somebody was saying beside him. Between him at one end of the room and me at the other there seemed to be a cleared way, as if everybody in the middle had drawn back to let us meet again.

It was just like a movie.

I looked at him, I hesitated, and then I looked at him again and set off. He didn't see me until I was nearly at his side. It was only the surprised glance of the person seated next to him that alerted him.

He looked at me. He didn't say anything. Neither did I.

I looked down at his impeccably dinner-suited knees and gave them a light precautionary brush as though they were a park bench.

Then I sat down.

He looked at me. He didn't say anything. Neither did I.
I looked down at his impeccably dinner-suited knees and
gave them a light press ... as though they were a
park bench.
Then I sat down.

CHAPTER 17

It was Vince who told me, as the new morning was breaking in
his hotel room, the final piece of news about *Elza's Story*. I was
lying in his bed still half-asleep when, predictably, I was woken
by the telephone. Vince moved across the bed to answer it.
When I stirred he reached out and drew me over to him while
he continued talking. We stayed in this position, gathered up
together on one small portion of the mattress, one of his arms
around me and the other free to hold the mouthpiece, both of
us half-propped up and entwined as if embracing on a narrow
ledge.

By the time he put down the phone I felt sufficiently confident to ask something I'd been wondering about.

'You didn't seem at all surprised to see me last night.'

'It seemed inevitable,' he answered. 'I'd heard you were here
and then last night Stuart was telling me all about the latest developments with *Elza's Story*. To me, you and the great Latvian
masterpiece have always been a package. You appeared in my
life at the same time. So when I looked up and saw you ...

'Mind you,' he laughed, 'I did think at the time that considering Stuart had just been to a screening of my film and was
now attending a reception for it he could at least have said a
few words to me about it ... but who am I? He went on and on
about the Great Work and what had happened in Moscow, how
when the word came down that they were releasing *Elza's Story*
at Cannes there was a great panic to do the French subtitles—
apparently they couldn't find a French-speaking Latvian—and
how he saved everything for them by telling them how great
your subtitles were, so they just switched them into French!
End of drama. They'll elect him Tsar at the rate he's going—'

He stopped because I had suddenly sat up. I was feeling cold. My hands began to shake. I had to swallow hard to clear my throat.

'You're certain?' I asked. 'You're sure he said *my* subtitles?'

'Sure,' Vince replied. 'Absolutely. That was the centrepiece of Stuart's great long story—'

'I can't believe it,' I interrupted, 'I can't—'

I had been about to leap up out of the bed but I could see that the time had come for the truth. It is hard to tell a complicated story for the first time. Vince was still looking puzzled as I ended my account of my rewrite of *Elza's Story*.

'It sounds like you did a great job,' he said.

'But does Balodis know?' I exclaimed, raising my voice. 'We have no idea of what's been happening in the last year either to him or to Leblenis.'

'Films are getting rewritten and re-edited all the time, you know that—' Vince began.

But I cut him short. I threw away the sheets and jumped out of bed. 'I have to be sure,' I said. 'I have to go and see the film.'

I wasn't the only one to be worried. Vince too, as he went with me to the Festival's cinema complex, was uncharacteristically silent. He would look at me as if about to speak and then obviously change his mind and look away frowning. As we walked along the street, he reached out for my hand. It was mid-morning now and the day was bright and hot, but I noticed as our fingers clasped that both our hands were cold.

The auditorium was huge, layer upon layer of people rising up, all crowded. We took our seats. Vince put his arm around my shoulder.

The credits began. Immediately my mind went back to the last time I'd seen *The Story of the Year of 1912 in the Village of Elza Darzins* at the preview screening in Sydney. At that time, after my first nervousness I'd sat and watched calmly as on the screen the actors said one thing in Latvian while in the subtitles I'd frequently have them saying—in English—quite another.

The credits were now over. We were in that cold bare room in Riga in 1950 and the aged survivors of Elza's village were together, remembering their past and, inevitably, regardless of how many other memories they raised, going back to this one event. The murder of the old schoolteacher, Elza's father, in 1912.

I knew that I had changed scarcely any of this section, so I tried to concentrate on aligning my limited knowledge of French to see if the French subtitles fitted the Latvian. I could recognise names and dates here and there; but it was not sufficient for me to feel any confidence that these were, exactly, my subtitles.

Then we reached the start of 1912: we were at the meeting of the committee set up to organise the celebrations of the Romanov accession.

I told myself that I must be imagining things. I reminded myself that it was a year since I had seen the film and that even *I* could forget every convolution of that complicated plot, but I sat forward listening intently, staring at the French subtitles, trying to establish if it could possibly be true? Could the Latvian *on the soundtrack* really be what I was beginning to think it was? Could the Latvian soundtrack be *a translation of the English subtitles I had written*?

I was unable to believe it—until we came to Elza's first grand performance as the village's resident philosopher. I heard her confidently start her monologue with 'as Prince Kropotkin says'.

These were *my* words. At exactly that same point I'd always heard Elza begin her speech with equal confidence with 'as Karl Marx says'.

Vince had laid a comforting hand on my back as I sat forward in my seat.

'It's all my dialogue,' I said.

'What?'

I didn't blame him for not understanding.

'They've re-dubbed the whole film,' I whispered. 'They

re-scripted it according to my subtitles. It's a completely new soundtrack.'

Then I reached out for his face in the dark and gave him a kiss.

He started to laugh, then kissed me back and drew me into his arms. Behind us there was a sharp urgent whisper in French. We got the gist. People like us should stay at home and make love.

Other people were here to watch the movie.

COPYRIGHT

Copyright © Thea Welsh 1990

First published in 1990 by Simon & Schuster Australia

This edition published in 2021 by Ligature Pty Limited
34 Campbell St · Balmain NSW 2041 · Australia
www.ligatu.re · mail@ligatu.re

e-book ISBN: 9781922749369

All rights reserved. Except as provided by fair dealing or any other
exception to copyright, no part of this book may be reproduced or
transmitted in any form or by any means without permission in
writing from the publisher.

The moral rights of the author are asserted throughout the world
without waiver.

ligature untapped

This print edition published in collaboration with Brio Books,
an imprint of Booktopia Group Ltd

Level 6, 1A Homebush Bay Drive · Rhodes NSW 2138 · Australia

Print ISBN: 9781761282065

briobooks.com.au

MIX
Paper from
responsible sources
FSC® C008194
www.fsc.org

The paper in this book is FSC® certified.
FSC® promotes environmentally responsible,
socially beneficial and economically viable
management of the world's forests.